T0149453

FATHER,
OH FATHER

FATHER, OH FATHER

B. RAE GREEN

FATHER, OH FATHER

iUniverse books may be ordered through booksellers or by contacting:

iUniverse
1663 Liberty Drive
Bloomington, IN 47403
www.iuniverse.com
1-800-Authors (1-800-288-4677)

ISBN: 978-1-5320-3254-7 (sc)
ISBN: 978-1-5320-3255-4 (e)

Library of Congress Control Number: 2017913833

Print information available on the last page.

iUniverse rev. date: 10/30/2017

This book is dedicated to

My daughter, Tracy and my son-in-law, Chuck,

My two handsome grandsons, Garrett and Jacob,

And my grandpuppies, Punkin' and Mo,

And my grandkitty, Misty

And my new great-grandpuppy, Milo

I also dedicate it to my Aunt Nancy,

My dear friend and cohort

And to those who keep me young,

The young men who are friends

With my grandsons.

It's a zoo around here at times,

But I love it.

PROLOGUE

MY NAME IS Odessa Sue Stanton. What a dumb name! Not Stanton. That's ok. It's the other two names that are dumb. Odessa Sue. Who, in his right mind, names an innocent baby Odessa Sue? My parents did. Although, who's to say they were in their right minds? Don't get me wrong. I love my parents very much. I just think they're a little strange.

Well, back to my name. My friends call me Ode, pronounced Odie. My dad calls me Odessa and my mom calls me Odessa Sue. Always. I don't think I've ever heard her call me just Odessa. It's always Odessa Sue. Somehow that just seems to make it worse. And here's the kicker. My initials are OSS which most older people think stands for the Office of Strategic Services which was known from World War II. So I even feel ridiculous using my initials. I can't win.

I am growing up on a farm in Ohio. The only thing different about it from other farms was that we don't do the farming. It is my grandfather's farm, and we just live there. My grandfather rents out the fields to another farmer who lives down the road. My dad works in a factory, and my mom stays at home to take care of me and my two brothers. I am the oldest and my brothers are ornery pests. As an example, my brother, Tom, at the age of two, rode his tricycle down the basement steps. He almost hit the concrete wall, but he turned at the last minute. But, I digress.

I am in a local college, and my brothers are still in high school. Since money is tight, I still live at home. At least that is the excuse. I really like living at home.

My best friend Judy lives down the road from me in a big three-story brick house. This is one of the biggest houses in or around our small town. The first floor is made up of a kitchen, formal living room, a parlor, and a bath. The rest of the house is bedrooms. It has been in the Winslow family for many generations and hasn't been updated very much. So, it still has a feeling of the Victorian era. Fortunately, the kitchen and baths are fairly modern.

Judy's full name is Judith Ann Winslow, and she is the only person who calls me Dessa, which I actually like. Her parents are rich, but Judy is down-to-earth, just like me. Her father is a nice man and a good father. Her mother is more like *her* mother.

When Judy's Grandmother Mitchell is around, everyone gets a lot straighter. Not just in posture, but in attitude. It is amazing how you can just see the difference.

Judy and I have been best friends since we were old enough to remember. We went all the way through school together and are now going to college together, too.

I have dark hair with hazel eyes, while Judy is a blue-eyed blond. She is cute and petite, while I am a little bigger and average-looking. We are both popular in school and get along with our classmates. The fact that Judy's parents have money never gets in the way of anything. In fact, we were soon to find out that we were going to depend on that money very much.

CHAPTER 1

ONE SATURDAY MORNING I was studying in my bedroom when Judy called me. "Dessa, please come over. My mom wants me to go up to the attic and straighten up and dust and sweep. Come over and help me."

"Judy, I'm studying for my test on Monday."

"If you come and help me, it'll only take half the time, and then I'll come over there and help you study for your test. Please?"

She always knows how to get me to agree to anything. I didn't care, though. We were best friends, and she would have done the same for me. "Ok. I'll be right over."

"Why are we doing this? I'm sure your attic is probably cleaner than most people's living rooms."

"My mom can't stand to have dust in the house. That includes the basement and the attic. I'm the one who has to do the attic. Pretty much all we have to do is dust the boxes, replace the sheets on the furniture and sweep the floor. Let's fold up the sheets first and set them out on the landing. Then we can dust and put the clean sheets on. The last thing we do is sweep. We also have to straighten up anything that looks out of place. We should be able to finish up in about two hours."

"Well, let's get started then."

They carefully took off the old sheets, folded them, and put them on the landing. When they were through, they would take them downstairs, shake them out, and put them in the laundry.

Then they started dusting the boxes. They came to a stack of boxes that somehow had gotten stacked a little too high. Judy said, "I think we should take some of these off the top. I don't know how they got like this. They weren't this way the last time I was up here."

They reached up as high as they could. They had to stand on their toes to reach the top box. They were lifting it down when, all of a sudden, the box started to tip. Neither one of the girls could stop it from falling onto the floor. Suddenly there were papers all over the place.

As they stooped to pick them up, Dessa noticed that the papers were some kind of legal papers.

Judy said, "I wonder what these are."

Dessa said, "I think we should just put them back and forget about them."

"Well, I'm going to read them," said Judy.

As Judy read, she gasped and said, "Dessa, look at these. They're about me. It says I was adopted by my dad."

They kept on looking through the box of papers and started putting the story together. Judy couldn't look any more. She started to cry.

Dessa was trying to put two and two together and finally said, "Judy, this is what I'm getting out of this. Your mom was married before she married your dad. They were divorced when she was pregnant with you. Just a few months after you were born, she married the man we call your dad. He adopted you. I guess they didn't tell you because they didn't think you'd ever find out about this." Looking up and seeing the tears running down Judy's face and the look of shock, Dessa leaned over and put her arms around her. "Hey, it's going to be ok. It really doesn't matter. You're still you. That hasn't changed."

"Yes, but I have a real father out there somewhere," sobbed Judy. "Do I look like him? Do I sound like him? Do I have other grandparents or aunts, uncles and cousins? Why, I could even have brothers and sisters. Now that I know about this, how can I just forget about it?"

They found Judy's parents downstairs in the living room. Rushing into the room, Judy waved the papers around. "Mother, Father. I found these papers in the attic. I want to know what's going on."

Odessa tried to back out of the room, feeling like an intruder, but just as she was about to make her escape, Judy turned and said, "Dessa, don't you dare leave me. There's no reason for you not to be here."

"Judith, what *are* those papers you keep waving around in my face?" said her mother in the voice that would have stopped Dessa cold.

But, Judy wouldn't back down. Dessa could see that she was trying to keep from weeping. Judy said to her father, "These papers say that you aren't my real father. Who are you then? And where *is* my father?"

Judy's mother had turned quite pale, but tried to bluff her way out of things. "Judith, this *is* your real father. I don't know what you think you know, but…"

"Margaret, stop. It's time to tell her the truth. I told you we should have told her years ago. Don't make it harder than it already is. Girls, sit down. Margaret, tell them the truth."

Gathering her wits about her, Margaret started telling Judy the truth, "You're right, Judith. The man who you have called Father all your life, is really your step-father. I was married before. When I was a young girl, I fell in love with a wonderful boy. Of course, my parents didn't approve of him, but I didn't care. I loved him very much and we ran away and got married. He was a good husband, but he didn't have much money or prestige, since he had grown up in an orphanage. That's why my parents didn't like him. They always wanted me to marry Alexander Winslow. Well, at the same time I found out that I was going to have you, your father found out that he had cancer and didn't have very long to live. My parents convinced him that it would be better for everyone if he left me." At this point, she looked to her husband, who gave her a smile.

"Alexander loved me, too, and still wanted to marry me. My parents gave your father enough money to go off and find a place where he could die in peace and his family could go on with their lives. He took the money and left and my parents pulled strings and arranged a quiet divorce for us. By the time I found out about all of this, it was too late. Alexander knew the whole story and since he still wanted to marry me, I did the best thing I could for you and went through with it. The stress of losing my husband, the new marriage, the betrayal of my parents and the birth of you was almost more than I could bear."

Alexander stood behind Margaret's chair and lovingly squeezed her shoulders.

Margaret continued, "I loved your biological father, Judith, but I put thoughts of him out of my mind. By the time you were born, I was sure that he had died. I learned to love Alexander and I haven't regretted one day with him." She squeezed his hand and went on.

"He said that we should tell you, but I just couldn't stand to bring the subject up. So I kept putting it off. And now.…. I'm sorry, Judy. Can you ever forgive us?"

Judy was softly crying as her mother was speaking. "I have to think about this. I'm going to Dessa's house for a while. Please just let me have some time."

"Judy, wait," said Alexander. "I need to tell you something." As he was talking, Alexander had gone to his desk and found a stack of letters. He brought them over to her, sat down beside her and put his arm around her. "First of all, I want to tell you that I have loved you always. It didn't matter that I wasn't your biological father. You were my little girl. I want you to remember that. Now I have to unburden myself by giving you these letters. Even your mother doesn't know what I'm about to tell you.

"Your father isn't dead." There were gasps from all the others. "He somehow beat the cancer. He wrote me and said that he didn't want to confuse you since you had a new life. He sent me a letter for each one of your birthdays. I wasn't to give them to you until the day came when you found out about him. So, here they are. I'm sorry, darling. We never meant to hurt you. You go on to Dessa's and we'll talk soon – when you're feeling a little better."

Judy hugged him, took the letters, then she and Dessa left the room.

As the girls left, Dessa noticed that Judy's mother still seemed in shock over the announcement that Alexander had made. She just sat there with silent tears running down her cheeks and her husband talking to her quietly, with his arm around her, trying to comfort her.

CHAPTER 2

A S DESSA WALKED into her house, she yelled, "Mom, Judy is going to be staying with us for a few days."

Her mom yelled back, "That's fine, Odessa Sue. Judy, you know you're welcome anytime for as long as you want to stay."

"Thank you, Mrs. Stanton," yelled Judy as she followed Dessa up the stairs.

When they got up to Dessa's bedroom and closed the door, Judy plopped down in Dessa's overstuffed chair. Odessa, being the only girl in the family, had the biggest bedroom (next to her parents that is). She and her mother had fixed it up so that it was warm and cozy. Besides the chair, there was a double bed, dresser, and desk. They were all in a beautiful mahogany wood which matched the woodwork. They had painted the room a soft green and accented the bedding in the same color. They also found a large carpeting remnant that matched the green, and Dessa's mother had made matching curtains for the windows. Dessa's dad had built on a bathroom and closet for her, too. That was her sixteenth birthday present. She spent a lot of time in her room, because she loved it so much.

Dessa stared at the letters in Judy's lap. Her friend looked up and said, "I guess I should read them."

Dessa said, "I'll go downstairs so you can have some privacy. Is it ok to tell my mom what's going on?"

"Of course. I know she'll understand."

"Ok. You call me when you're ready for me to come back up." With that, she left the room and went downstairs to talk to her mom.

When she went back to her room, Dessa noticed that Judy's face was white as a sheet. You could tell she had been crying, but had somewhat composed herself.

Dessa sat down on her bed and waited until Judy was ready to talk to her. When she was ready, she said to Dessa, "My father loved me. When he wrote the letter for my eighteenth birthday, he told me the whole story about his disappearance. My grandparents *did* pay him to leave, and since he thought he was dying, he took the money and left. He said he went to a cancer center in Florida. He has a rare blood type, and that's why they thought he would die. The doctors didn't think they could find a match for him in time to treat him. But this hospital in Florida performed a miracle. A match dropped into their laps. At least that's what he said. But by the time he recovered, it was too late."

Taking a deep breath, Judy continued, "My mother had remarried and I was born. He didn't want to wreck my life by coming back. He did hope that one day I would find out the truth so he started writing the letters. He secretly contacted Alexander who agreed to keep the secret. And you know the rest." She paused for a minute and then said, "Dessa, I have a father out there someplace and I need to find him. He said he moves around a lot and that it would hurt my mother to try to find him, but I must. And, you have to come with me. I don't want to go alone."

"Judy," began Dessa, "we just can't leave school and go running around trying to find someone who doesn't want to be found. That could take a long time. Maybe you'll *never* find him."

"Dessa, listen to this. It's from the most current letter. The one from my twenty-first birthday." Judy started reading,

'My dear daughter,

I am writing this letter for your twenty-first birthday. As they say, time flies. Just yesterday I was picturing you as a little girl. Now I must get used to seeing you as a young woman. A beautiful one, of that, I'm sure. I don't know if you're in school or are working at the career of your choice. I'm sure that you excel greatly at whatever you do.

I want you to know that I am still cancer-free and feeling fine – even for an old man. At least, I'm sure that's how you must think of me.

I want to tell you again (as I do in all the other letters) how much I love you. You will always be, in my heart, my darling baby girl.

Love and kisses,
Your Father

As Judy finished the letter, she folded it, and carefully put it back in the envelope. When she looked up, Dessa sighed and said, "Ok, I give up. I'll go with you. We'll figure things out, somehow."

CHAPTER 3

A S HE PUT the letter into the envelope and sealed it, Jack Woodley sighed and looked around the room that was his. It was the typical motel room that he had lived in all his life. There was scratched paneling on the walls and faded, worn carpeting on the floor. The ceiling had been lowered and the panels had places that showed there had been a water leak at some point in time. There was a window air conditioner that put out luke-warm air. The furniture had seen better days, but at least the bed was comfortable. The one thing that was to the room's benefit was that it was clean. He could tolerate its shabbiness because of its cleanliness. Not all of them were.

Jack put on his jacket, put a stamp on the envelope, and left the room to go to the mailbox in the lobby of the motel. It, too, was shabby but clean. The man attending to business was old and tired-looking. He looked like he had been in the same spot all of his life. But, he was friendly enough, and his smile was warm.

He looked up as Jack opened the door. Showing that warm smile, he asked, "How can I help you, Son?"

Jack, smiling back, said, "I want to send this letter. Can I do that here?"

"You sure can. The mail man will be here soon, so you're just in time." He took the letter and put it on the stack of others that was going out. "Can I help you with anything else?"

"No. I'm good. Just on my way to work," he said. And, with that, he went out the door and got in his fifteen-year-old pickup truck to make his way to the club.

He was the lead singer in a band. Not a great band. But they were good enough for him to make it through life as long as he didn't try to live too high on the hog. He had no responsibilities other than himself, and he didn't require much to live on.

The drummer, Gene Evans, was his best friend. They had started the band together with three other guys. After all these years, they were the only two left of the original group. They always managed to replace the ones who left with suitable people, but it would have made the band better if they could keep the same five people for longer than a few months.

He got to The Club early. He never bothered to find out the name of where they played, because he knew they would be moving on, and he'd just have to learn a new name, again. So he always called them "The Club." That saved his memory for more important things. Now, he just had to decide on some more important things.

There weren't many people in The Club yet, but that was ok with him. He wanted a cup of hot coffee and a few quiet moments to himself. He didn't smoke, and he had been sober for ten years. He didn't stay in one place long enough to develop a relationship with anyone, even if he could find a decent woman in the areas where they played. So, his vice of choice was coffee. He drank so much that sometimes he thought his stomach sloshed. But, that didn't matter as long as he stayed sober.

He looked around the room and decided that it looked pretty much like the rest of the places he played. It was dark and would soon be smoky when the patrons started arriving. There was a stage and a small dance floor. The tables and chairs looked like they had come out of the prohibition days. The bartender was a good-enough man, but he wasn't the friendliest person around. The waitress who was usually there, was a little too friendly. She wore too much makeup and too few clothes. Ever since they started playing there, she had been trying to get him to come up to her room with her. That was never going to happen, but he wasn't in the habit of hurting a person's feelings, so he kept putting her off as nicely as possible.

As he finished his second cup of coffee, the rest of the band showed up. He got up from the table, put his empty cup on the bar, and went to the stage to get ready for tonight's show. Maybe a miracle would happen and something exciting would happen tonight.

CHAPTER 4

THE CALL FROM Judy's mother asking them to come back to the house was more of a command performance. When the girls walked into the living room, it was a shock to see Judy's grandmother sitting there. Dessa couldn't help thinking that she didn't look as menacing as usual.

Because it was expected of her, Judy went to her grandmother and gave her a kiss on the cheek. Then Judy and Dessa sat down and waited for someone to speak.

Finally, Judy's mother said, "Tell her, Mother."

"Don't press me, Margaret. This is difficult enough. I need to gather my thoughts." Victoria took a deep breath and began. "Judith, your parents have told me that you found out about your biological father. I do regret that you found out the way you did. It was never the intention of your grandfather and me to hurt you. We never thought you would find out about all this. I thank God that your grandfather passed without knowing how hurt you are. And, as your father told you, we never realized that your biological father was still alive. That is quite shocking to me, considering how sick he was. Judith, I don't know that I have ever said this to you. I love you, very much. Your grandfather did, too. You have always made us very proud. I hope you can forgive us for our part in the deception." Victoria stopped speaking and slumped, noticeably, in her chair.

Judy looked at Odessa with a look of pure surprise on her face. Getting up, she again went to her grandmother and gave her a hug and kiss. "Thank you, Grandmother. I can see that that wasn't easy for you.

Yes, I can forgive you. I'm sure you thought you were doing what you thought was best, at the time." Sitting back down, she then addressed everyone in the room. "I forgive all of you, but you have to understand that I can't let this go. I need to find him. Father, it doesn't change how I feel about you, but Dessa and I are going to find him."

Margaret started to speak, but Alexander stopped her and said, "Judy, I can understand how you feel, and your mother and I will do whatever we can to help you. I will give you all the information I have and will support you both, financially, until you are satisfied. Is that all right?"

Now it was Judy's turn to go to her father. He enveloped her is his arms and hugged her closely. "Thank you, Father. I will make sure that you and Mother know where we're at so that you don't worry about us. I'll also make sure you know what progress we make."

"I know you will. Now, why don't you, Dessa, and I go into my office and go over the details. We'll leave your mother and grandmother to their tea."

"Ok, Father." Dessa got up, while Judy went to her mother and hugged and kissed her, and told her g randmother good-bye.

Walking into the office, Dessa could feel the hair on the back of her neck stand up. Whether it was from excitement or fear, she couldn't tell.

CHAPTER 5

NOTHER EVENING WAS over at The Club. It had been a normal evening. By that, Gene meant that there were no drunks heckling them and no fights had broken out. He was getting too old for nonsense like that. Oh, he had done his fair share of fighting in his youth, but it finally got through his head that using your fists settled nothing and only made you hurt. So, unless someone came after him or one of the band members, he stayed out of it.

The guys were always hungry after they got through at The Club and there was always a Diner just down the street, across the street, or around the block. This one was across the street. It was amazing how the crummiest-looking diners usually served the best food. So, across the street they went as soon as they packed up their gear for the night.

This diner had a meatloaf dinner that was to die for. Well, those are words you should never use in the same sentence as diner, I guess. It was really good. So the band had a standing order and the Diner always made sure that is was ready, waiting, and hot when they got there.

As the band sat down at the big round table in the corner, Stella (who always waited on them) started them off with their coffee and then brought their food. The younger guys started gobbling their food down, but he and Jack had learned to appreciate good food. So they sat together and talked while they ate.

Looking around at the dingy diner, Gene asked Jack, "Did you mail the letter?"

"Right on time. Don't I always?"

"Yeah, but you're getting older. You could have forgotten."

"Look who's talking about getting older. You're right there with me, pal," said Jack.

Grinning sheepishly, Gene answered him back with a jab to the ribs.

Jack said, "So, what are we going to do on our one night off tomorrow night?"

"Well, we could go out drinking and chasing women, or we could catch a movie like we usually do on our night off."

Dennis, the newest band member, overheard this exchange between the two and started snorting with laughter. "Boy, you two are something else. I thought guys your age knew how to party. You're sounding like an old married couple. What's up with that?" he asked.

Laughing with Dennis and the others, Gene answered, "Ok, guys. We've had our day of parties. We just like to play our music and live a nice, quiet life. We'll leave the partying to you young bucks. The only thing we ask is don't get in trouble doing it. We don't have the money to be bailing any of you out of jail."

While they were all laughing about this, Stella brought over a piece of cherry pie for each of them. Pie at this place was the highlight of the meal, so there was only the sound of forks scraping up the juicy goodness and stuffing it into their mouths until every bit was gone. Then they sat back with contented sighs, finished their coffee and finally unwound from the evening.

After that, they went back to their rooms for a good night's..er.. day's sleep.

CHAPTER 6

ODESSA AND JUDY were on their way to Florida. According to the information given to them by Alexander, which he had attained from Victoria, that was where Judy's grandparents had sent her father to get treatment. They had promised Alexander that they would drive carefully, stop at dinner time for the night, and stay at reputable hotels. By following these rules, it took them four days to get to Miami. Alexander had reserved a suite for them in one of the best hotels and told them, again, to take as much time as they needed. He had also transferred plenty of money to their hotel account and they would use what they needed and take with them any that was left over.

As the girls approached the reception desk, the woman behind the counter looked up and smiled. Smiling back, Judy said to her, "Hello, my name is Judith Winslow, and there should be a reservation in my name for a suite. There, also, should be a cash account in my name."

"I'll check for you. Just a moment, please," said the woman whose name tag called her Caryn. Checking her computer, she told her, "Yes, Miss Winslow, your father has arranged everything. Please, sign in, and I'll have someone take you to your suite, right away." As the girls signed in, Caryn called for a bellhop to take them and their luggage to their rooms.

Once they got there, and the bellhop left (with a generous tip), Judy turned to Dessa. "What should we do now?"

I think we should unpack and call room service for dinner. While we're waiting on that, we could take our showers, get into our pajamas, eat, and spend the rest of the evening relaxing. It's probably the only time we'll be able to do that for a while. Then tomorrow we can get an early start by going to the hospital. I agree with your father that we should take as many meals as we can in our room. How does all that sound to you?"

"Wonderful! The only change I want to make is this. Can we sleep in? We've been on the road for days, and as much as I want to find my dad, I'm tired."

"Yes. I feel the same way. Now, let's unpack so we can order dinner. I'm also starving."

After room service had taken away the empty cart that had once held two delicious steak dinners and apple pie ala mode, the girls settled down in the living room in front of the TV. Alexander had spared no expense to make sure that they were comfortable. The bedrooms were large with beautiful furniture. Each bedroom had its own bathroom which any girl would give her eye teeth for. The living room had a long couch which could have seated a half-dozen people, easily. There were two recliners in a soft leather and the tables around the room were in a cherry wood that looked like antiques, not just old. The colors on the walls in the suite were soft but charming. Dessa found the carpeting to be not only beautiful, but so thick and soft that she could have slept on that as easily as sleeping on the bed.

After watching TV for an hour, the girls decided to go to bed and get a good night's sleep. After all, they were starting tomorrow on what could be a long journey.

CHAPTER 7

AFTER GETTING THAT good night's sleep, the girls got ready while they were waiting on their breakfast. After eating, they went down and got in the car.

Since Dessa was driving, Judy was the navigator. Judy gave her the address, checked the local map, and they were on their way. Dessa wasn't used to the crowded streets, so she drove carefully.

After about twenty minutes, Judy told Dessa the hospital was just ahead on the left. They parked the car, got out, and walked inside to the attendant.

Judy asked, "Where would we go to find a former patient?"

"You can go to patient records, but that information is usually considered privileged. Take the elevator to the seventh floor, room 703. I'll let them know you're on your way. May I have your names, please?"

After giving her this information, they found the elevators, and made their way to the seventh floor. Knocking on the door a pleasant voice said, "Come in." As they entered the room an older woman with silver hair motioned for them to take a seat. "My name is Mrs. Haver and you must be Miss Winslow and Miss Stanton."

Judy said, "Yes, I'm Judith Winslow and this is Odessa Stanton."

"How can I help you?" asked Mrs. Haver.

Taking a deep breath, Judy told Mrs. Haver the story that had been relayed to her. When she finished, there was quiet in the office.

Mrs. Haver finally broke the quiet. "Miss Winslow – Judy, I wish there was something I could do to help you. Normally, patient records are not available to anyone. I will talk to my boss about your circumstance, but it seems to me that your father doesn't want to be found. So I'm not even sure that any judge would give a court order to open them. Let me know where you are staying, and if there is anything that can be done, I will call you. But don't get your hopes up."

Unable to speak, her hopes dashed, Judy got up and turned to leave. Dessa turned to Mrs. Haver and said, "Thank you for your time, Mrs. Haver. I guess we'll just have to try something else." She reached out and shook Mrs. Haver's hand and turned to follow Judy out into the hallway.

Mrs. Haver turned back to her work, with a sad look on her face. Talking to herself, she said, "I wish I could have helped that poor child."

Lucky for Dessa, she was able to find her way back to the hotel without too much trouble. She was concerned about Judy, who sat thoughtfully, quiet, next to her. When they got back to their room, Dessa expected Judy to fly off the handle into a tirade. But, instead, she didn't say anything and just started pacing the living room. Dessa didn't say anything to her. She just sat and watched her pace, until Judy finally stopped and looked at her.

"If she thinks that this is going to stop me from finding my father, she is crazy. Let's get food. I'm starving."

Dessa called room service and ordered soup and sandwiches for lunch. Then she sat back and waited to see what plan Judy would come up with.

CHAPTER 8

D ESSA AND JUDY had finished their lunch and were discussing what their plan of action was going to be now, when there was a knock on the door. Dessa went to answer it, and there was a young woman standing there holding a briefcase and a large file. The woman had blond hair and striking, green eyes. Dessa thought her to be about the same age as her and Judy.

The woman said, "Are you Judy Winslow?"

"No, I'm Odessa Stanton." Just then, Judy came up and stood beside Dessa. "This is Judy."

"My name is Wendy Thornberry."

"How can we help you, Miss Thornberry?"

"Why don't I come in and explain it to you. It seems to be a little complicated."

Dessa said, "I'll get us some coffee from room service. Would you like anything else, Miss Thornberry?"

"No, that will be fine."

While they were waiting for the coffee, Wendy said, "Please, call me Wendy. And you are Judy and Odessa."

"Judy calls me Dessa, so you might as well, too. I'm getting the feeling that we are going to get to be close friends."

"Yes, I think you're right. I'm a private investigator. And before you say it, I am too young to be one, but none the less, I am one."

Room service interrupted them. After the waiter left, they settled back with their coffee.

"I was in my office when these files were messengered over from someone at The Cancer Hospital. There was a note included that had your names and hotel on it. I glanced at the file, but it didn't make a lot of sense to me, so I decided to just come on over and find out what the deal was. Here, Judy, I guess these were meant for you." Wendy handed all the paperwork over to Judy, who was looking amazed.

Judy and Dessa looked at each other and said, at the same time, "Mrs. Haver." Seeing Wendy's confused look, Dessa filled her in on what had happened at the hospital.

Judy said, "I think we're going to need help. My father will pay for your services, Wendy. I need to find my biological father. Are you in or not?"

"This is the most exciting case that I've had since I started in this business. I'm in."

"Good. Since you're the professional, what's our next step?"

"Let's divide these records up between the three of us and see what we can find."

For the next few hours, the three women perused the hospital records of Judy's biological father searching for any clue as to where he might be now. Finally, Wendy spoke up.

"The only thing I can find – and this might be a stretch – is that there was a donor. It doesn't say who this person was, and it might not even help to know. But, that's all I have. What about you two?"

"I don't have anything. What about you, Judy?" asked Dessa.

"No, nothing. For what it may be worth, we have to try to find this donor."

"I have a few friends at the hospital. I'll see what I can get from them," said Wendy. "There is the possibility that the donor is dead, but if not, we'll find him…or her. You two just stay put and I'll get back to you." As she got up to leave, Wendy put her hand on Judy's shoulder and said, "Judy, I would give anything to have my father back. I can only imagine what you must be going through. I'll do everything I can to find yours."

After Wendy left, Judy called home to give her parents an update on what they had found. Her mother answered the phone. "Mother, how are you?"

"Oh, Judith, it's so good to hear your voice. It seems so lonely without you here. Are you still in Florida?"

"Yes, we are, and it's beautiful down here. But, I miss you, too. I just wanted to call and let you know how things are going." Judy went on to tell her mother what had happened so far. When she finished, she said, "That's all so far. I love you and Father. Would you call Dessa's parents and tell them we're all right?"

"Of course I will. We love you, too. Call again soon, darling."

"I will, Mother. Good-bye."

When Judy hung up, Dessa asked her, "Why don't we put on our bathing suits and go down to the pool? We can tell them, at the desk, where we will be, in case Wendy calls."

"We might as well." Pausing, Judy finally said, "Dessa, do you really think Wendy can help us get this done?"

"I know she thinks she can. That's a good start."

CHAPTER 9

T HE BAND HAD finished their two weeks in Mesa, Arizona. They had eaten their last dinner at The Diner and were off to the next gig. This one was in Goodyear, their last stop before they got to California. It wasn't a long drive, only about an hour. It took them longer to get their equipment and personal items packed in the trailer than it would take them to get there. After loading up the trailer, Dennis, Peter, and Tim piled into their beat-up van and took off. The van, like Jack's truck, wasn't the best-looking van, but between Jack and Gene, they were able to keep it running well.

The drive to Goodyear was uneventful, and when they got there, they went directly to The Club to drop off their equipment. While this one was similar to the one in Mesa (and other places they had played), it was in a little nicer neighborhood.

Walking in, Jack said to Gene, "Since we're going to be here for two weeks, I'm glad to see this place is in better condition than most of the places we play. Maybe, we're finally on our way up."

Laughing, Gene replied, "You just keep thinking like that. I love a positive attitude. Maybe the Big Guy will hear you."

"Nothing's impossible, pal. Now, let's get busy and get this stuff set up. We need to go get us our luxury living quarters. I'll go check with the bartender and see what he recommends."

Before Jack had a chance to go to the bar, Dennis came up to them and said, "Hey, guys. I'm sorry to have to do this to you, but I have to leave the band. I don't really want to, but I got a call from my mom, and she said my dad had a heart attack. It's not a bad one, but my mom needs me. I've already packed up my stuff and I'm getting a flight out in a couple of hours."

Jack and Gene gave Dennis their condolences and best wishes. After Dennis had gone, Gene asked Jack, "Well, now what?"

"Now, I go over to the bartender, ask him about a motel, and a new band member." Going over to the bartender, Jack said, "Hey, Bubba, we're in kind of a fix. I hope you can help us. First, we need a cheap, but decent motel. The next one is a little more difficult, but very important. Our bass guy had to go home and we need someone to replace him. One who can go on the road with us. I don't suppose you have someone behind the bar, do you?"

Bubba laughed and said, "Well, you're right. I can help you with the motel. There's a place out on W. McDowell Road. It's called Murphy's Motel. I know the owner, Mike. If you want, I can call him and tell him you're gonna need some rooms."

"That would be great. I'd appreciate it. Now, how about that guitar player?"

"Now, that may be a bit trickier. Why don't you go get your rooms taken care of and call me back in a couple of hours. I'll see what I can do for ya."

"Ok, Bubba, will do. Thanks," said Jack.

Jack went back to Gene and told him about the conversation with Bubba.

Gene said, "Let's get Peter and Tim and head for Murphy's. I think I'll take a nap and dream about a new bass player."

Jack went to his room after leaving Gene to take his nap. He planned on settling in and wait until it was time to call Bubba. Opening the door, Jack was glad that he had taken the bartender's advice on where to stay. This room was pretty nice. Not only was it clean, but it had been taken care of. While it certainly wasn't fancy, Jack knew that Mike Murphy cared enough about the place to keep it pleasing to the eye. The room had been painted recently in a soft yellow. The carpeting wasn't new, but it was in good shape in a brown that went well with the walls. The furniture included, not only a double bed, but a recliner (one that actually worked), a dresser that you could feel comfortable putting your clothes in, and an unbroken mirror. Jack checked the bathroom and found everything to be in working order. He decided to watch a little TV before he unpacked and found that the remote worked, too. The time they stayed here was going to feel like heaven. If only they could all be this nice.

He watched TV for a while and then unpacked the few belongings he had. By then, after looking at his watch, he found it was time to call Bubba. As he dialed, he prayed that he was going to hear good news.

When Bubba answered the phone, Jack said, "This is Jack Woodley. Have you got good news for me?"

"As a matter of fact, I do. One of my waitresses knows a bass player. She'll be here a couple of hours before show time to meet with you."

"She?" Jack sounded surprised. He had never even considered they might be hiring a female. "Well, Bubba, beggars can't be choosers. We'll be there."

CHAPTER 10

WHEN THE PHONE rang, Dessa answered it and heard Wendy's voice saying, "Dessa, this is Wendy. I'm starving and I have some news. How about meeting me at Angelo's for dinner? I'll be there at six. Just tell your taxi driver the name. Everyone in this area knows where it is and it's only ten minutes from where you are." Barely waiting for a reply, Wendy hung up.

After telling Judy about their dinner plans, Dessa said, "I'm going to take a shower first. Then we can go."

"I'm going to take one, too. Do you think she's found out something important?" Judy asked.

"Well, she sounded excited, so I'm hoping she did."

They both got ready and went downstairs. They took a cab that was waiting out front and gave the driver the name of the pizza parlor. Wendy was right about the driver knowing where to go. She was also right in that it took only ten minutes to get there. Judy paid the cabbie, and they went into the restaurant.

Looking around for Wendy, Dessa noticed that they were in a typical pizza parlor. The tables had the usual red and white checkered table cloths with the wax-covered, Chianti-bottle candles in the center. They had gotten there ahead of Wendy, and although the place was busy, they managed to find a booth in a corner, where they would have a little bit of privacy.

Judy waved when she saw Wendy come in and look around for them. She hurried over and sat down. "I'm starving. Let's order and then

I'll tell you what I found out." They gave the waitress their order for a large pepperoni and mushroom pizza and three Coca-Cola's.

Having done that, Wendy took a deep breath and said, "I found the man who was the donor to your father. His name is Charles Bradburn. He owns a major pharmaceutical company in Miami. I thought we could go see him tomorrow morning."

"Of course, we can. I'm sure he will know something about my father," said Judy excitedly.

"Great," said Wendy, "I'll pick you both up at nine tomorrow morning." Just then, the waitress put their steaming-hot pizza on the table. "Let's eat and celebrate another step to victory." The girls put their glasses together and dug into the pizza.

The next morning, Wendy was right on time. Dessa and Judy were ready and waiting for her. Judy looked as if she hadn't gotten a lot of sleep the night before – which she hadn't.

When they got in their car, Wendy gave them directions to the Bradburn Pharmaceutical Company, and then sat back and looked at Judy. "It's going to be all right. Just let me ask the questions. And try not to look so scared or overly anxious."

They found a parking garage a few blocks from the building. They walked to the Company and went in, and Wendy gave their names to the receptionist. When she said they were there to see Charles Bradburn, the woman gave her a quizzical look. She picked up the phone and quietly exchanged words with someone. When she hung up, she turned to them and said, "You may go up to the executive offices now. Take the express elevator, and give them your names. Someone will be waiting for you and get you to the right office."

As they got into the elevator, Dessa turned to the others and asked, "Did you get a feeling that something strange just happened? She was acting awfully funny."

"I thought so, too," said Judy. "I'm starting to get a bad vibe about this."

Wendy said, "Now, let's not get ahead of things. Here we are. Just take a deep breath."

When the doors opened on the floor of the executive offices, there was a young woman in a navy business suit and matching high heels, standing there waiting for them. She had a strained smile on her face, but she greeted them warmly. "I'm Miss Hensley. Are you ladies here to see Mr. Charles Bradburn?"

Wendy said, "Yes, we are."

"Please follow me." She turned and led them down a wide, beautifully decorated hallway.

As they followed her, Dessa murmured to Judy, "I can see now why drugs cost so much. This hallway alone is worth a small fortune. Do you see the paintings on the walls? Wow!"

Miss Hensley led them to an office at the end of the hallway. Knocking on the door, she then opened it and stood back to let them in. She left, closing the door behind her.

In comparison to this office, the outer reception area looked like a dump. The walls were paneled in a beautiful, dark mahogany that had a high, gloss finish. The carpeting was soft and thick and the color of the ocean. There was a huge fireplace at one end of the room, surrounded on each side by floor to ceiling bookcases. They were filled not only with books, but lovely vases, statuettes, and other small collectibles. Done in a rich, cocoa brown leather was a couch and two large chairs in front of the fireplace. The tables at each end of the couch and the coffee table in front of it were all antiques as was the large executive desk. The room would have been dark and gloomy if not for the large, floor-to-ceiling windows behind the desk area and at the end of the room.

Standing behind the desk was a man who looked to be in his late thirties. His suit, shirt, and tie were very expensive. He was smiling at them, but the smile didn't reach his eyes. They were cold and hard. That made him seem like a very intimidating man.

Motioning for them to sit down, he said, "My name is Joseph Bradburn. I know you're here to see my father, Charles, but I must tell you that he passed away a few weeks ago. I'm rather surprised that you didn't read about it in the papers."

"My name is Wendy Thornberry. I've been out of town and my associates are from Ohio. I'm terribly sorry to hear of your loss, Mr. Bradburn."

"May I ask, what the nature of your business with my father is? Maybe I can be of some help."

Judy nodded slightly at Wendy to give her permission to continue. "Mr. Bradburn, Miss Winslow has come to Miami searching for her father. He came down here from Ohio to get treatment at The Cancer Hospital. He thought he was dying, but a transplant saved his life. Miss Winslow has only just recently found out that she was adopted. This occurred about twenty years ago."

"Why, Miss Thornberry," asked Joseph, "did you want to see my father?"

"Because, he was the donor."

"You said this was about twenty years ago?" asked Joseph.

"Yes."

"Well, I would have been only fifteen at that time. I was away at boarding school, so I would have no knowledge of this. My father was a private man. He would have kept this information to himself. I'm afraid I can't give you any information because I have none."

Disappointed, Wendy asked, "Would your father have kept any records on something like this?"

"I've never run across any, but I would be glad to look. Leave your name and contact number with my assistant, Miss Hensley, and if I find anything, I will call you," said Joseph, standing.

Recognizing this as a dismissal, the girls stood up, too. Wendy extended her hand and said, "Thank you, Mr. Bradburn, for your time and help. We certainly appreciate it."

Joseph must have pushed a button under his desk, because as they turned to leave, Miss Hensley opened the door for them. They followed her out of the office. Wendy gave her the information that had been requested and they left the way they had come.

Meanwhile, Joseph Bradburn picked up his private line and placed a call. "Stanley, we've got a problem."

CHAPTER 11

D AISY DIXON WAS a cute, petite, baby-face blonde. Jack and Gene took one look at her and then at each other. They just shook their heads. They were screwed. The bass guitar hanging around her neck was almost as big as she was. At this point, they had no choice. So they went to the stage and introduced themselves.

Gene said, "Let's jam a little and see how things go. We'll start and you pick it up. I assume you can do that?"

Daisy gave him a disgusted look and said, "Let's get started, boys."

So they did. They started in and she picked things right up. They played another three songs, and they all sounded better than ever. She was the best bass player they had ever had.

Grinning broadly, Jack said, "Well, Daisy, I owe you an apology. You're great! I hope you can stay with us for a while."

Grinning right back, Daisy said, "I accept your apology, Jack. I'm in for the long haul, boss."

"Good. We're here for two weeks, and then we're off to California. Can you get away that soon?"

"No problem. All I have to do is pack, and I'll be all set."

Everyone in the band seemed to play exceptionally well that night. As the week went on, the crowds grew larger and larger. Jack and Gene were having fun. Daisy brought an excitement to the band that hadn't been there before. Even Peter and Tim seemed to pick up on it.

When the evening was over, Gene said to Daisy, "We always go out to eat after we're through. Would you like to go with us?"

"Thanks, but I've got things to do at home, since I'm going to be leaving soon. When we're on the road, I'll fit in with the rest of you. I'll see you all tomorrow."

Everyone said good night to her, and she left. The guys left to go eat. They had, of course, found the diner that they claimed as theirs. At least for the next two weeks.

When Daisy got back to her apartment, she was exhausted. The evening had gone well, and she was happy to be part of the band. It had been a long time since she had been in a group, and these guys were pretty good. Even though they had doubted her ability, they had accepted her fast enough when she showed them what she could do.

Raising her voice, Daisy said, "Cat, I'm home. Where are you?"

A voice coming from the back said, "I'm in my bedroom. I'll be right out."

By the time Daisy put her guitar down and took her jacket off, her sister, Catherine, came into the kitchen. She was in bright pink pajamas with a matching robe and slippers. She asked Daisy, "How did it go tonight?"

"Very well. They really liked me."

"Of course, they did," said Catherine proudly.

"I got the job. We'll be here for two weeks and then off to California," said Daisy with excitement.

Hugging her sister, Catherine said, "Well, the hard part is over. I knew you were good, but they might not have hired you for any number of reasons. I'll notify the boss and let him know that we have passed the first hurdle. The rest should be a piece of cake."

"Yes, I'm sure he will be delighted," replied Daisy.

"Daisy, you'd better take me with you tonight so that I can meet the band. We're going to have to break the news to them that I'm going with you. We'll stick with the story that you don't think it would be 'proper' for you to go on tour without me. Can you sell that one?"

"Of course, I can. They think I'm just a ditzy blond. It will make perfect sense to them. They might not like it, at first, but they'll get used to it."

CHAPTER 12

WHEN THEY GOT to the sidewalk, Dessa said to Wendy, "Did you get the same feeling that I did that there was something strange going on up there. I think we got what my Dad calls The Bum's Rush."

Wendy answered her, "I got the same feeling. He said he didn't know anything about the transplant because he was at boarding school. Yet, he didn't act surprised or ask us any questions about it. If I thought my dad had done something like that, I would certainly want to know more about it."

"So what are we going to do now?" asked Judy.

"I'm not sure," answered Wendy. "We're going to have to do some digging, because I don't think we're going to hear from Mr. Joseph Bradburn again."

As they started walking back to pick up the car, they didn't notice the limo pulling up outside the building they had just exited. The driver opened the door to let out a distinguished-looking, middle-aged man. He was ordinary looking, but he dressed well. He hurried into the building like he was on a very important mission.

Going directly to the express elevator, he waited impatiently for the doors to open. When they did, he entered and pushed the button for the doors to close. Getting off on the floor of the executive offices, he went directly to Miss Hensley.

"Mr. Bradburn is waiting for you, Mr. Nichols," she said. "Would you like me to take you to his office?"

"No, I know the way. I'd better get in there before he has a heart attack." Having said that, he turned and walked, hurriedly, down to Mr. Bradburn's office.

He entered, without knocking, and found Joseph Bradburn staring out the window. Without turning, he said, "Stanley, what kept you? We have a situation that needs taken care of – and with much haste."

"I got here as soon as I could, Joseph. Traffic was awful. So what is so important that I had to rush down here so fast?" He sat down on one of the chairs in front of the fireplace and crossed his legs.

Pouring them both a double Scotch, Joseph handed one of the glasses to Stanley and sat, facing him, in the other chair. Stanley nursed his drink, but Joseph downed his right away. Then he spoke. "I just had a visit from three young women. They were here to ask about my father's organ donation. One of the women was the daughter of the man Father donated to. I told them I didn't know anything about it, but I don't think that will satisfy them. The daughter is trying to find her father, and I don't think she is going to stop looking. You have to do something to make sure she doesn't find him. I've worked too hard to make sure he stays lost."

"Joseph, what do you want me to do about it?"

"Make sure she never finds her father."

"And just how do you want me to do that?" questioned Stanley.

"I think you know what I'm getting at."

Looking at Joseph with a shocked expression on his face, Stanley asked, "You want me to get rid of her? How am I supposed to do that?"

"I'm not going to get involved in the details. Just take care of it – and soon. This is the last I want to talk about it. Get it done. And Stanley, do I need to remind you that you falsified Father's will?"

"You know that wasn't my idea. It was yours." Stanley had grown even paler than when he came in.

"How would I know that the will you filed in probate wasn't real? After all, you're my father's attorney. I would have no reason not to believe you. Now get out of here and get busy."

Sighing, Stanley said, "All right. I'll take care of it." After Stanley was told the details needed, he got up to leave. As he reached the door, he turned and said to Joseph, "I hope this doesn't come back to bite you in the rump." With that, he left, shutting the door behind him.

Joseph stood and stared at the door after Stanley left. He then went to the bar and poured himself another Scotch.

Stanley Nichols was a good attorney. He was also a greedy one. He didn't like bowing to Joseph Bradburn's every whim, but he knew that with the conclusion of this assignment, there would be a huge reward. And he did like all that money. He knew enough people who could make this wish come true, and there would never be a tie to him. So on his way back to the office, he made several phone calls.

One of those calls was to a Vincent Maglioni. When Vincent answered the phone, Stanley said, "I've got a job for you. Listen carefully."

CHAPTER 13

BACK AT THE hotel, the girls decided to discuss their next move over lunch. While they were eating, Judy said, "I know that it seems like we've hit a wall, but the more we hit one, the more determined I am to continue on. What can we do now, Wendy? We aren't going to get anything out of Mr. Joseph Bradburn."

Chewing on a piece of celery, Wendy said, thoughtfully, "I have a feeling that there won't be any private information that we are going to be able to get. I think that has been hidden by Sonny boy. But, we should go to the library and get as much information as we can about Charles Bradburn. We might find something that will lead us to the information we need."

The girls finished their lunch, quickly, and headed down to the car. When they got to the library, they went to the front desk and asked for all the available data on Charles Bradburn and The Bradburn Pharmaceutical Company. The librarian showed them where to look and then left them alone.

Dessa said, "There's a lot here, but if we divide it up, it should be manageable."

For the next few hours, they looked through all the personal and Company data that there was. Finally, Wendy said, "I think I found something. Here is a list of employees of The Bradburn Pharmaceutical Company. It also lists their positions. It shows a Lucille Watkins was personal assistant to Mr. Charles Bradburn. What do you want to bet that as soon as Mr. Bradburn died, Ms. Watkins was no longer needed?

If she was his assistant long enough, she might have what we need. Let's see if we can find her."

Finding a phone book, Wendy said, "Keep your fingers crossed." She then looked up Lucille Watkins. "There are three in the book. Let's write down the numbers and addresses and go hunting."

They went to the first address, but the Lucille Watkins they found was a twenty-five-year-old, single mother of two small children. But at the second address, they hit pay dirt. The woman who answered the door looked to be in her mid-fifties.

"Are you Lucille Watkins?" asked Judy.

"Yes, I am. What do you want?" she answered.

"My name is Judy Winslow and these are my friends, Odessa Stanton and Wendy Thornberry. We're looking for the Lucille Watkins who was the personal assistant to Charles Bradburn."

"Yes, that's me. How can I help you?"

"We'd like to speak to you about a personal matter involving Mr. Bradburn. May we come in and talk to you about it?"

Hesitating a moment, she stepped aside and let them in. Leading them to the living room, she said, "Please sit down. Can I get you something to drink? I just made some lemonade."

"Yes, thank you. That would be nice." said Wendy.

While they waited for the lemonade, they looked around the living room. It was a clean room, but very minimalistic. There were no family pictures and only a few pictures on the walls, which were painted a pale sage green. The hardwood floors were covered in a coordinating rug. The furniture was fairly new and comfortable. What stood out the most was the brand-new console TV.

Just then Lucille came in with a tray of lemonade and some cookies. After handing everyone a glass and a plate, she said, "I notice you looking at my TV. It was a retirement gift." Pausing a moment, she looked at them with a trace of tears in her eyes and said, "Well, that's behind me. Now, how can I help you?"

Diving right in, Wendy said, "Judy is looking for her biological father. He came to Florida to The Cancer Hospital because he thought he was dying. But, he was fortunate enough to receive a transplant. The donor was Charles Bradburn. We went to the Company to talk to Mr. Bradburn and found that he had passed away. So we ended up talking to his son. His son told us that he knew nothing about the donation and that there was no information about it in any of his father's records. We don't believe him. That's why we came here."

Looking at Judy, Lucille seemed to struggle. Finally, she said, "Charles Bradburn was a kind man and a wonderful employer. I'm afraid that can't be said about his son. Mr. Bradburn…Charles, that is, had a rare blood type. He was registered at all the hospitals in the area, in case it was ever needed. One day, The Cancer Hospital called and said that there was someone with his blood type who needed a transplant and would he consider doing it. He went to the hospital and talked to someone there about it. When he came back, he called me into his office and said we needed to clear up some business, because he was going to go ahead and be the donor for the transplant."

Eagerly, Judy asked, "What else did he tell you about it?"

"That was all he told me. We got down to business then, so he could be gone for a week." Seeing the dejected looks on the three faces looking at her, she went on, "But, Charles was a firm believer in keeping detailed records of everything."

Now it was Dessa's turn to speak up, "But his son told us there were no records about this situation."

"Well, that's because he lied to you. There were records on a lot of things that he wouldn't want anyone to know about. But, I have made copies of a lot of things, and one of those is a detailed file on the transplant." Lucille then got up and went upstairs. She was gone for several minutes, and when she came back she had a thick file in her hands.

"This is everything that Charles had on the transplant. You'll find it quite thorough. Please take it. I know he would want you to have it." She then put the file on Judy's lap and sat back down, looking pleased. "This helps to make up for the fact that I was 'not needed anymore' after Charles died."

She put the file in her oversized purse. "Thank you, Lucille," said Judy, quietly.

"I'd like to ask a favor of you three," said Lucille.

Wendy answered, "Of course, what can we do for you?"

"I may be paranoid, but I don't believe that Charles died of natural causes. Oh, I know, that's what was said, but I don't believe it. He was in great shape and said he had never felt better. If you find out that his death wasn't due to natural causes, would you please let me know?"

"We would be very happy to let you know. We'll also let you know when we find Judy's father. I am sure that with your help we'll find him."

The girls got up to leave and gave Lucille, not only their thanks, but hugs as well.

When the girls left Lucille's house to go to their car, they were so excited to have the file, that they didn't notice the man in the car watching them. Calling on his phone, he said, "Yeah, they're coming out now. I don't know what the old lady told them. They're leaving now. They should be close to you in about ten minutes. Don't mess this up!"

CHAPTER 14

J ACK HAD NOTICED the young woman who was sitting by herself at a corner table. Usually he didn't pay much attention to the patrons of the places they played. But, there was something about this woman who stood out to him. The fact that she was alone would have been enough, but she didn't seem to be drinking very much or interacting with anyone else in the bar. The fact that all her attention was on the band didn't hurt anything, either.

The evening had gone well. Very well, in fact. Daisy was a great addition to the band, and Jack hoped that she would be with them for quite a while. When the band was done, they got their equipment put away and stepped down from the stage. He was surprised when Daisy went over to the woman who had been the focus of Jack's attention. The woman stood up and the two hugged each other. Daisy then took the woman's hand and half dragged her over to the rest of the group.

The woman looked embarrassed as Daisy said, with excitement, "Hey, guys, this is my sister, Catherine. She's my twin sister. She's going on the road with us."

At this, Jack and Gene looked at each other in shock.

"Daisy, you pick the worst times to make announcements," said Catherine, laughing at her sister. "As you can see, we're not identical twins. We don't look alike nor do we act alike – well, not always. What Daisy meant to say is that I'm going to be traveling with you, but I pay my own way. Now, I'm sure you're all hungry, so let's get something to eat – my treat."

So they went to their new favorite diner. Daisy, Peter, and Tim sat in one booth and started talking away about the performance that evening and the upcoming gigs. That left Catherine to sit with Jack and Gene in another booth.

When they placed their orders, Catherine made sure that the waitress knew she was paying for all of them. She then turned to the other two and said, "Well, this is awkward, isn't it?

Suddenly they all laughed and the air seemed to clear.

Gene asked her, "How can you take the time and the money to go around with Daisy?"

"Have laptop, will travel. My job allows me the freedom of doing it anywhere I can take my computer. Daisy seems like someone who is in full charge of her life, but, at heart, she still needs me. And, not trying to be personal, but I don't think it' s proper for her to travel, alone, with just men. So, I'm able to go with her. She should have talked to you to make sure it was ok with both of you. I'm sorry she didn't do that first. I hope it's okay. I promise not to interfere in your business. I'm just going to support Daisy – and all of you, of course."

The guys looked at each other, and Jack spoke up, "I guess we have our first groupie. Well, you have to start some place. Welcome aboard. There is one problem though. We don't have room for an extra person. It's pretty crowded as it is."

"That's ok. I will drive my own car. Daisy will ride with me, and if you need extra room for anything, you can stash stuff there."

Gene spoke up, "Now if you can just get us some gigs that last more than two weeks, you'd be perfect."

Laughing, Catherine said, "Well, miracles happen all the time. We'll have to see about that, too."

Their food came about that time, so they all dug in. As usual, they had picked the right place to eat. Talk died down while they ate, and after homemade peach pie, Catherine paid the bill, and they got up to leave. After Daisy hugged everybody, she and Catherine left to go back to their apartment. The rest of them went back to their motel. Peter and Tim went to their rooms and Jack and Gene stood outside their rooms to talk for a minute about their new situation.

"I don't know about you, but I would have never seen this coming.

First, we get a female who plays a mean bass guitar. Then, not only does she have a twin sister, but that sister is coming on the road with us. And, she seems to have money. Are we going up in life or down?" said Gene, shaking his head.

"I'm with you. I would have never dreamed of this. I guess we just go with the flow and see how things play out. For right now, though, I'm going to get some sleep. Good morning."

"Yeah, me too."

But, as Jack laid in his bed with his hands supporting his head and looking at the ceiling, sleep eluded him. He couldn't help thinking about Catherine and how different she was from Daisy. Finally, though, he drifted off, still thinking of her.

He slept well, but realized that when he woke up, she was the first thing on his mind. "This can't go on," he mumbled to himself as he was getting ready for the day. "You've got to get her off your mind." Then he went back to his usual routine – without Catherine.

When they went to play that evening, he found that he was disappointed to find that Catherine wasn't going to be there. He tried to casually ask Daisy about her sister. "Will Catherine be joining us this evening?"

Daisy answered, "No, she's getting things ready at home for when we'll be gone. She's the organized one. I'm not. She thinks she's still a girl scout – be prepared and all that." She then went to the stage to get herself ready for the first set.

Shaking off his disappointment, Jack, too, went to the stage to get ready. Was it his imagination or did everyone seem more light-hearted than before. They were even playing better, too. This might work out after all. Only time would tell.

CHAPTER 15

DRIVING BACK TO the hotel, the car was full of chattering. All the girls were so excited about the file they had gotten from Lucille.

"I will be so glad to get back to the hotel so we can dig into this file," said Judy. "It is going to lead me to my father. I'm just sure of it."

Suddenly, as they were preparing to stop at the next intersection, there was an explosive sound and Dessa lost control of the car. She tried to stop for the red light, but slid right into the intersection. They were then hit by cars coming from both directions. There was the noise of screeching brakes, metal slamming into metal, and screams from pedestrians witnessing the disaster. Pieces of the cars were flying about, people were scattering, and cars were piling up.

Inside the car, there were screams as well, while Dessa was trying, desperately, to control the car and keep it from sliding into traffic. When she realized that she couldn't, bracing herself was the first thing on her mind. Everything seemed to happen in slow motion. She saw the cars coming at them. Then she saw Judy's head hit the side window and the blood streaking down. She had no idea what was going on with Wendy, who was in the back seat.

Finally, after what seemed like hours, everything stopped, and there was quiet for a brief moment. As quickly as it had started, it ended. The accident had taken less than a minute.

Dessa was stunned and groggy. Moving her arms and legs, she thought she was okay, with the exception of a bruising she felt from the steering wheel. She looked over at Judy. Gently shaking her, Dessa found her to be unconscious, but breathing. She turned to see about Wendy. Wendy had a shocked look on her face, but Dessa thought she looked all right, otherwise.

By this time, she heard the sounds of sirens – lots of sirens. There was the police, ambulances, and even the fire department. People were getting out of their cars and going to other cars to see how everyone was. Finally, the EMTs came to their car, along with the fire department. Their doors had to be pried open. When they were, the EMTs insisted on putting collars around the girls' necks and placing them carefully on back boards. Judy was rushed to a waiting ambulance, since she still had not regained consciousness. It took off with lights and siren on, running at full speed. The other two girls were taken to another ambulance which left at a more reasonable speed.

Fortunately, they were all taken to the same hospital. Dessa and Wendy, while shaken up, only had some bruising. They were both treated and released. Judy, however, had a slight concussion and a cut above her eye. She had a sprained wrist, too. The emergency-room doctor said, "We're going to keep your friend overnight. Her concussion isn't that bad, but we would rather be cautious. We've moved her to a private room, and you can go see her."

Dessa and Wendy went to Judy's room and found her awake, but quiet. "Are you two all right?" she asked them.

Dessa spoke first, "Yes, we are. How do you feel?"

"Other than a headache, I don't feel too bad. Did you call my parents?"

"No. We thought it would be better if you called them. That way they would know you were okay. Here's the phone."

Judy dialed the phone. Her mother answered on the first ring. "Hello."

"Mother. It's me."

"Oh, Judith. It's so good to hear from you. But, you don't sound like yourself. Is everything all right?"

"Well, not exactly, Mother. We had a car accident and I'm in the hospital. Mother, please don't cry. I'm okay, really. I'm not sure what happened. Let me give the phone to Dessa. She knows more about it than I do. I just wanted to let you know that I was all right. Here she is." With an apologetic smile, Judy handed the phone to Dessa.

"Hello, Mrs. Winslow. This is Dessa. First let me tell you that Judy is going to be just fine. She has a sprained wrist and a slight concussion. She's only in the hospital overnight as a precaution."

"Odessa, what happened? What kind of accident were you in?"

"The tire on the car had a blow-out. We were at an intersection and got hit by another car." Dessa had decided to play down the accident as much as possible so as not to scare Judy's parents any more than she had to.

"Are you all right, dear? Maybe Mr. Winslow and I should come down there to be with you girls."

"Other than a few bruises, I'm all right. Wendy, the private detective we hired was with us. She only got minor bruising, too. And I don't see why it would be necessary for either one of you to come down here. We'll stay the night with Judy and take her back to the hotel tomorrow. I promise you that we will rest for the next few days. I'll make sure that Judy calls you when she gets back to the hotel. I know we can handle things at this end."

"Well, I guess we'll do as you say, Odessa. Please call if you need us for anything. Anything, at all. Should I call your mother for you?"

"No, thank you. I'd better do that myself. We'll be talking to you soon. I promise."

Dessa had no more than hung up when two men came to the door of Judy's room.

The first man to enter the room was middle-age with dark hair and gray at the temples. He was of average height and in fairly-good shape, showing just a little bit of a paunch. The other man was younger and taller. He had dark brown hair and a great build. Both of them had kind faces. When they walked into the room, the older man said, "I'm Detective Jacoby and this is Detective Barlow. We're with Miami PD." Detective Barlow pulled out a notepad and flipped it open and pulled out a pen so he could take notes. "Are you three Odessa Stanton, Judith Winslow, and Wendy Thornberry?" When the girls all nodded yes, he continued, "We're here about the accident you were in."

Wendy decided to take the lead by saying, "I'm Wendy Thornberry, Detectives, and I'm a licensed private investigator here in Miami. I'm going to cut right to the chase. Why are they sending out two police detectives for a car accident? Granted, it was a bad accident, but it could have been worse. All this over a blown tire? What's going on?"

"You're right, Miss Thornberry. We certainly wouldn't be here for just a routine car accident. Your tire didn't just simply blow. It was shot out." He waited while he watched their faces go pale. "I don't think you realize how lucky you all were that you're not dead. The way those cars hit you was unbelievable. If they would have hit your car differently, it would have been completely crushed – with you in it. Now what we want to know is who would want to kill you and why?"

Again Wendy answered, "If our tire was shot out, how do you know it wasn't meant for someone else and whoever did it was a bad shot?"

Detective Barlow answered this question by saying, "The shot came from a 22-250 Savage rifle. Anyone using that would hit what they were aiming at."

"Miss Thornberry, you said you are a private investigator. What case are you working on and what does it have to do with these young women?" asked Detective Jacoby.

"Now, Detective, you know I can't answer that. And, these young women are my friends. They came to Florida to visit me on their vacation. I don't think there is anything else to tell you. I think you should leave now. Judy needs some rest. We appreciate your concern. If there is anything else we can help you with, we'll be in touch."

The detectives handed her their cards, said their good-byes, and turned to leave.

Detective Barlow said, "Miss Thornberry, remember you all could be in great danger. Please be careful."

When they left, Wendy went to the door and looked out into the hallway to make sure they had gone. She then shut the door and leaned on it while looking at Dessa and Judy. They were all quiet for a couple of minutes until Dessa finally said, "Do you think they were telling the truth?"

Wendy answered, "Yes, I think they were. Which means there is more to this than just finding your father, Judy. I'm not sure what it is, but I'm glad we grabbed your bag that had the file in it and didn't leave it in the car."

"We need to go over this file with a fine-toothed comb but not until Judy can do that with us. Right now, she needs rest. Judy, you need to go to sleep. We'll be here all night. We're not going anywhere," said Dessa.

"Yes, I am very tired. Please take good care of the file." Judy then closed her eyes, and despite the excitement the detectives caused, was asleep within seconds.

Dessa and Wendy settled in for a restless night. They each dozed off for a little while, but never at the same time.

The only activity in the room that night was the nurse coming in to check on Judy. The next morning, the doctor came in and declared Judy well enough to be dismissed. The nurse brought in the discharge papers for Judy to sign. After that, she got dressed and they left the hospital.

Wendy said, "I already leased us another car. It's in the parking lot next to here. I also think you should check out of your hotel room. I know of a place outside the city that we should all go to. We need to stay together. I believe safety in numbers to be more than just a saying."

There being no dissent between Dessa and Judy, they found the new rental car and took off for their hotel. When they got there, the valet took the car, and they went to their room to pack.

"Judy, you sit down, rest, and hang on to that file. Wendy and I will take care of the packing. Oh, you could call down and get us checked out."

Wendy added, "If you think we can manage the bags, I'd rather not have a bellhop. The fewer people we come in contact with, the better."

"Sure we can. Judy, have them bring the car around, too."

Dessa and Wendy made quick work of packing their bags. By that time, Judy had them checked out. They took the elevator downstairs, stowed their bags in the trunk, and, with Wendy driving, they left for their hide-away.

Driving for about twenty minutes, they finally pulled up to a modest-looking motel. Pulling up to the office, Wendy said, "You two stay here. I'll check us in."

She went into the office, where a heavy-set, motherly-looking woman sat behind the desk. Looking up when she heard the bell over the door ring, a huge smile came to her face. "Wendy, sweetie, it's good to see you," she said.

"It's good to see you, too, Aunt Ginny. I wish I could say this was a pleasure call, but I'm here on business."

"How can I help you?"

"I need to rent the cottage." In back of the motel was a small cottage that was kept for special guests. It was out-of-sight from the motel and would be perfect for the three of them.

"It's yours for as long as you need it, honey. Here's the key. I assume that since you need the cottage, you're not here if anyone asks?"

Leaning over the counter to give her aunt a kiss, Wendy said, "Nothing gets by you, does it? Thanks, Aunt Ginny. I love you."

"I love you, too, sweetie."

Wendy went back to the car, got in, and drove around the motel to a dirt driveway that led back to the cottage. She explained to the other two where they were going and who owned the cottage. When they got there, they got their bags out and went to the door. Wendy opened it and they went in. The walls in the whole cottage, except for the kitchen, were painted white. But it was anything but boring. There was color everywhere – in the pillows and throws on the furniture, and the pictures on the walls. The bedrooms had colorful bedspreads with matching pillow shams. There was carpeting on the floor here, and beautiful hard-wood floors in the rest of the cottage. The kitchen was painted golden yellow, along with the table and chairs. The whole cottage was a cheery place for them to stay.

They had stopped at a local grocery store and had enough food and supplies to last them for a week. Wendy said to the others, "I'll take the food into the kitchen and put it away. Can you get all the bags taken upstairs?"

Judy said, "Yes, we can. I'm feeling much better now. So, no problem."

"Ok. You two take the bedroom with the twin beds and I'll take the other room."

Once they got everything put away, they made lunch and settled in the living room to eat. Judy pulled the file out of her bag. "There's enough folders in here that we can each go over some. Let's get started."

CHAPTER 16

"MR. BRADBURN, MR. Nichols is here to see you. He doesn't have an appointment."

"That's all right, Miss Hensley. Tell him to come in."

Waiting for Stanley Nichols to enter the room, Joseph walked to the bar and poured himself two fingers of Scotch. He downed it quickly and poured another for himself and one for Stanley.

When Stanley entered the room, Joseph motioned him to sit down. Handing him the drink, he said, "What have you got to report? Are they dead?"

Clearing his throat, Stanley said, "No. Apparently the plan didn't go quite as well as it was supposed to. Their tire was shot out, and their car was hit by two other vehicles, but luck was with them. The girl looking for her father got a concussion and a sprained wrist. The other two just had some bruising. Their car was totaled. I can't believe they got out of that alive. They spent the night in the hospital but got out the next day. They then checked out of their hotel, but by the time our man got there, they were gone. We haven't been able to locate them yet."

The further Stanley got in the story, the redder Joseph's face was getting. When he got through giving all the details, Joseph said in a voice that was overly quiet, "I thought I could trust you to hire people who could take care of this for me. But, all I'm hearing from you is failure. Do you know how much money I'm going to lose if this girl finds her father and they figure out what's going on? If I lose one dime, I can guarantee you will lose everything. I'll make sure of that."

"Now, Joseph, don't worry. They will be found and taken care of. I promise you."

"Again, I will take you down if you don't take care of them. That's my promise to you. Now get out of here and get busy."

CHAPTER 17

"JUDY," SAID DESSA. "We've been reading for three hours and everything has been technical stuff. I don't understand a third of what I've read."

"I've got the same problem," added Wendy.

"So have I. Let me see if there's anything else in this folder." Judy picked up the folder and looked inside. Putting her hand in to feel around, she suddenly felt some paper bunched up in the bottom. Pulling the papers out, she smoothed them out on the coffee table. Picking them up, she glanced at them and got an excited look on her face. "These seem to be something personal written by Charles Bradburn. I'll read it to you."

Today is the day that I have looked forward to but never thought would ever come to pass. I got a call from The Cancer Hospital. They want me to come test to be a donor. I am anxious to do this.

I did the test and everything matches up with the donee's bloodwork. The transplant is on. I'm excited, but I don't want to tell anyone about it except Lucille. She is a wonderful secretary. So loyal. She will keep my secret. I am glad that Joseph is away at school. I can't tell him about this. I know he will not understand. After all, he is only fifteen. Too young to understand and even if he did, I don't believe he would approve. Strange that I should care what a fifteen-year-old boy should think.

I'm here – in the hospital. Tomorrow is the big day. I will be giving a part of me to someone who could die without it. Somehow it makes running my company a very small thing in comparison. I know it's not true, but I will feel like such a failure if this doesn't work. I must get a good night's sleep. Tomorrow….

The transplant is done. I am up and running again. Now we will have to wait and see how our young patient does. The nurses say he appears to be doing well up to this point.

It has been several weeks since the transplant. The young man is doing quite well. He has recovered better than had been hoped. I must admit something. I have been very curious as to the identity of him. We are supposed to be strangers to one another. That is a silly thing. He owes his life to me, and yet he cannot know who I am? What nonsense!

Although I have tried never to use my wealth for anything but good, I have decided to use it to get something I want very badly. I don't know what is going on in my heart, but there is a great need for me to know the identity of the young man I have helped. I assisted a nurse in her need to extinguish her student loan debt. In return, she gave me the name of the young man. I then hired a private investigator to get more information on him. I am now waiting for his report. I get more anxious by the minute. I can hardly conduct the business that I need to attend to because of it. Luckily, Lucille helps to keep my focus straight.

The report has come. It sits on my desk, and I just stare at it. Afraid to open it lest it not say what I want it to say. Finally, I gather up my courage. You fool, are you afraid of a little piece of paper? Opening the envelope, the words blur as I see what I have been hoping for. The young man whose life depended on me is my son. The baby who was taken from me by his mother. I never knew of him for years, because of her thinking I wouldn't want them. How mistaken she was. By the time I found her, she was on her deathbed and had given the boy up for adoption. I lost track of him, but now I have found him again. Thanks be to God for this glorious miracle.'

Looking up from the pages, Judy said, with glistening eyes, "I can't believe it. Charles Bradburn was my grandfather. That makes Joseph my uncle."

"I have a feeling I know who is after us," said Wendy. "I think that Joseph Bradburn knows all about this and is threatened by your father and you. I think that both of you have a claim to the Company that

Joseph has been claiming as his own. It must be worth millions, and little Joey doesn't like to share. Go ahead and finish reading, Judy. Then we can decide on a plan of action."

Judy, again, picked up the papers and started reading.

'I sent Lucille to the hospital to extend an invitation for my son to come here to meet with me. I didn't tell him who I was or why I wanted to see him. I will tell him that when he gets here.

When Lucille got back from the hospital, she informed me that my son will, indeed, come to the office. She said he told her that he is guessing that I'm the donor. Whatever makes him come here is all right with me.

He's here. In my office. Sitting across from me. I can see the likeness to his mother and me. He has her beautiful eyes and my nose and mouth. What a nice-looking young man. I can't wait any longer. I tell him who I am. Why did I have to blurt it out like that? He looks so shocked – disbelieving. I show him a picture of his mother. He studies it. He recognizes her. At last, he believes me. We go to the easy chairs and sit across from one another. We talked for hours. He has no bitterness in him. Not for either his mother or me. I want to introduce him to his brother, but decide not to. I want him all to myself for now. He tells me that I have a granddaughter and the circumstances surrounding her. I have offered him a part of the business equal to that of Joseph's. Maybe then he could be involved in his daughter's life. But he declines. He only wants to pursue his musical career. He loves his child, but doesn't want to disturb her life. My son is a very responsible man. Oh, how I love him. He doesn't want anything from me, but I insist on giving him some money to start him off in his career. He had recently met another young man and they were starting their own band with three others. They wanted to tour the United States. I have to let him. When he got up to leave, we both had tears in our eyes. We hugged and said our good byes. He thanked me for his life. When he went to the door, he turned and looked at me for what I knew would be the last time. I don't know why I thought that. It was just a feeling in my gut. I've learned to trust that feeling, so I etched his face in my memory. I love you, son. Good-bye.'

Judy looked up at the two others and said, "That's all there is. He sounds like he was a wonderful man. I wish I could have known him."

"I'm sorry you weren't able to, Judy," said Dessa. "But, at least, there's still the hope of finding you father. That's what we're going to have to figure out how to do."

"Now, we've got to get busy. But, I think we've had enough for today. Judy, you look tired. I think we should let this go for now. We'll make dinner together and then get some rest. Tomorrow we'll get started full force. OK?"

The other two nodded in agreement, and they all headed to the kitchen.

CHAPTER 18

AFTER BREAKFAST THE next morning, Wendy said, "I think I can get this started. Judy, can we get any pictures from your mother? Or could she work with someone who could sketch a likeness of your father?"

"No. My grandparents got rid of any pictures they had of him. And I can't ask her to go through what it would take to draw him. This has been really hard for her. I've already asked enough of my family. We're going to have to do this without them."

"The only other person we know who knows what your father looks like is Lucille Watkins. I'm going to call my friend Wally, who is a sketch artist at the MPD. He can do wonders, and I'm going to set up a time for Lucille and him to get together."

"But, Wendy, she saw him twenty years ago. He may not look anything like he did then. So how is this going to help?"

"Wally is a genius. He has the skill to age a picture of anyone. Twenty years is nothing to him. I'm going to call them both now and see what we can do."

Wendy picked up the phone and called Lucille first. "Lucille, this is Wendy Thornberry. I have another favor to ask of you."

"What is it Miss Thornberry? Didn't the file help you?"

"Yes, it did. And we thank you very much for giving it to us. The hospital records don't have a name on them – only a patient number. We don't have a picture of the man we're looking for, either. We need to know what he looks like, and, as far as we know, you're the only one we can ask, who has seen him. Do you think you could describe him to a police sketch artist?"

"I don't know if I even saw him good enough at the time. And, that's been twenty years ago. My memory isn't that good, Miss Thornberry. I'm not sure I can do this."

"Would you be willing to try? Please? It's really important."

There was silence on the phone for a minute. Then Lucille said, "I guess I could try. But, I make no promises."

"That's fine. Whatever we get will be better than what we have now. I'm going to call the artist and see how soon he can come out to see you. I'll call you back as soon as I find out something." Hanging up the phone, she told the girls that she had gotten the ok from Lucille. Picking the phone back up again, she dialed her friend, Wally.

When Wally answered, Wendy poured on the charm. "Hey, Wally. This is Wendy. How are you, my friend?"

"Ok, I recognize that tone of voice. What do you want?"

"Now, Wally, can't I just call you to say hi?"

"You could, but you never do. What do you want?"

"All right, you win. I do need your help. I'm looking for someone. He's the father of a friend. She didn't know about him until a few weeks ago. There's a woman we know who knows what he looks like. We need you to draw him from her memory."

"What's the catch, Wendy?"

"It's a twenty-year-old memory."

"Boy, you don't ask for much, do you?" Wally asked sarcastically. "What else?"

"I need you to go to her. This involves some important people, and I need to keep it quiet. Can you meet me there in two hours?"

"All right, but you owe me big for this one."

"You got it, Wally." She gave him the address of Lucille's house and called Lucille to let her know the plan.

Wendy met Wally outside Lucille's home. When they walked up to the porch together, Lucille met them at the door. Once inside, Wendy introduced Wally to Lucille.

"Hi, Lucille. Let's sit here on the couch and I'll explain what we are going to accomplish. Wendy, we're going to be fine."

Lucille said, "Wendy, there's lemonade and cookies in the kitchen if you'd like some."

"Thanks, I think I will. I remember how good they were the last time I was here." Wendy wandered out to the kitchen and found the glasses. She poured herself some lemonade and grabbed a couple of cookies. She decided to go outside and sit for a while. Lucille had a beautiful yard with a cute patio set. She sat down and picked up a magazine that was laying there. The weather was perfect for sitting outside.

Wendy idly turned the pages of the magazine, not really looking at them. She was thinking about Judy and how she was an indirect heir to a huge pharmaceutical company. And, if her father was dead, that made her a direct heir. Somehow, she didn't think Joseph Bradburn was ever going to let that happen. Her father wasn't a threat to his brother – until now. If he was reunited with his daughter, that might make a difference in how he felt about the business. The only thing she could do was to find Judy's father, reunite the two, keep both of them alive, and expose Joseph Bradburn. Nothing to it. Yeah, right!

After about an hour-and-a-half, she went back in to see how the picture was shaping up. She took her glass, rinsed it out, and put it in the dishwasher. She went back to the living room, and Wally looked up with a crooked smile on his face. "We should be done in just a few minutes. Lucille has remembered more than she ever thought she would."

So Wendy went to the front window and looked out while waiting for them to finish up. Suddenly there was a flash of light as the sun hit a metal object in the car that had pulled to the curb across the street.

Screaming at Wally and Lucille to get down, she pulled her Glock 41 out of its holster strapped to her leg. She ran to the door as shots rang out and the front window shattered. Running into the street, she fired after the car that had rapidly pulled off down the street. She was too late to even get a good look at the license plate.

She turned to go back into the house and found Wally running out with his weapon drawn. "It's too late, Wally. They're gone. Is Lucille all right?"

"Yes, just shaken up. You weren't kidding when you said this case involved some important people."

They went back in the house to find Lucille with a broom, cleaning up the glass from the window. Wendy went to take the broom from her hands. Lucille looked at her with wide eyes and a death grip on the broom. Wendy managed to pry it out of her hands and lead her over to the chair. Wally handed Lucille a glass of water. She had started to shake by that time.

Wendy kneeled down in front of the chair and said to Lucille, "This was no accident. Someone doesn't like it that you are giving me information about this man. We need to get you out of town – and fast. Do you have any family that you can stay with for a while?"

"Yes. I have a cousin who lives in Maine. I could go stay with her for as long as I need to. But, what about my house? I can't leave it like this."

Wally spoke up then, "I have someone who'll come and fix the window. I have a lot of friends who will also make sure that nothing happens to the house while you're gone."

Wendy looked gratefully at him and said to Lucille, "Would your cousin have a problem if you just popped in on her? I don't want you to call in case someone is tapping your phone."

"No. She's been asking me for months to come up and see her."

"Then go upstairs and pack your suitcases. Write down her address for me, and I'll make the arrangements to get you out of town."

While Lucille was upstairs, Wally made some calls to his friends. He then said to Wendy, "You need to go back and make sure your friends are ok. I'll make arrangements to see that Lucille gets to Maine safely. Then I'll get back to the station and finish up with this picture. I'll fax it to you. Let me know if I can do anything else for you. I assume you want all this kept quiet?"

"Yes, I do." Going to Wally, Wendy put her arms around him and gave him a big hug. "Thanks, Wally. I really owe you big time."

Grinning, Wally said, "You sure do."

CHAPTER 19

J ACK FOUND THAT when Catherine was in the audience, he played and sang much better than when she wasn't there. He wasn't sure why that was. She didn't treat him any differently than she did any of the other band members. Maybe he was going through a mid-life crisis, and this was how it was manifesting itself. Oh, well. As long as he kept his thoughts to himself, he wasn't making a fool of himself.

Saturday night drew a large crowd. Word had gotten around town that their band was very good. At dinner afterwards, Daisy said, "Cat, since we're off tomorrow night, why don't we fix these guys up with one of our picnics and go to the park. Please? We haven't had a picnic in a long time."

"Well, fellas. How about it? Daisy's right. We haven't had one for a while. And we cook some mighty good food, if I do say so myself."

Peter said, "I think that's a great idea. Let's. It beats going to the movies again."

So they all agreed that they were going to have a picnic. Jack said to Catherine, "You shouldn't have to do all the cooking for all of us. That doesn't seem fair."

"Ok, let's do it like this. We'll cook and you guys can bring the pop and beer. How about that?"

"That sounds better. Give us directions to the park and we'll meet you there about one o'clock. Will that be good?"

"That will be perfect. Just make sure you guys bring your appetites. Daisy and I are great cooks."

"Never fear. That's one thing we never forget to bring," said Jack, chuckling.

At exactly one o'clock, the guys pulled into the park and found the girls easily. They had put two picnic tables together and topped them with bright, red-and-white, checkered table cloths. On top of them were dishes of potato salad, baked beans, cole-slaw, tossed salad, potato chips, dinner rolls with butter, and fried chicken. For dessert, there was apple pie and chocolate cake with plenty of chocolate frosting.

The guys pulled a large cooler out of the truck. It was filled with pop, beer, and water. They had also brought a Frisbee, some baseball gloves and balls.

Gene said, "Did you girls get any sleep? You certainly have outdone yourselves with the food. I'm even hungrier than I thought I was. If it's half as good as it looks, we're in for a treat."

Daisy, grinning from ear to ear, said, "Making this was nothing. Cat and I work pretty fast. Besides, I have a confession to make. We really had this planned out before last night. So we had a lot of the food already made. I don't know what we would have done if you guys didn't agree to this."

They all laughed at Daisy and the look of contrition on her face. She wasn't very good at looking sorry. She never was. "Come on. Let's eat!" And so they did. Everyone was quiet as they ate the feast that had been prepared.

After they had managed to fill themselves completely, Peter, Tim, and Gene pulled Daisy to her feet, grabbed the Frisbee, and ran over to an open spot to throw it around.

Jack said, "Do you want to go play Frisbee or toss the baseball for a while?"

"No, I think I'll just sit here, let my food settle, and enjoy this lovely weather."

"Good. That's exactly what I wanted to do, too." He opened a beer for each of them while Catherine spread a blanket on the ground. They sat down and drank their beer. They watched the others throwing the Frisbee and just enjoyed the quiet, peacefulness of the park.

Finally, Jack said, "It's hard to believe that you and Daisy are twins. You seem more like her mother than her sister."

"Our father died when we were three. Our mother had to work two jobs to take care of us. I always took her place when it came to Daisy. When we were twenty, Mom died. Daisy would have been lost without me. We love each other dearly. Without me, she would be broke in two weeks and out on the streets. I have to keep her feet on the ground most of the time."

"It sounds like a rough life."

"We never thought of it like that. It's just the way things were. I don't think I would have had it any other way. With the exception of the death of our parents, that is. Now I have a good job, and we can live quite well. That is, we don't have to worry about having a roof over our heads and food on the table. Now, enough about me. What about you?"

"I've lived a boring life. I grew up with a mother, father, and younger brother. My dad went to work every day, and my mom stayed at home and took care of her family and the house. When I was twenty-one, I met Gene. We started a band, and the rest, as they say, is history."

"It doesn't sound so boring to me. It just sounds normal. You love your music. I can tell. Not everyone can do what they love. Boring would be you going to an office every day. You'd hate that."

"You're a wise woman, Catherine Dixon. Thanks for putting things in the right perspective for me."

The others ran over just then and prevented any further conversation between the two of them. They were all starving again. Gene sat down on the blanket with a beer while the rest of them hit the food table again.

"Jeez, I'm getting too old to be playing with the kids," Gene said. "I think I'll just hang out with you two, if you don't mind."

"Of course we don't mind," said Catherine. "So, Gene, we've been talking about our past lives. Tell me your story."

"Well, before I met Jack, I didn't really have a life. When I met Jack, then I started to live. The band means everything to me. Jack and

I built it together and, you might say, it's our baby. We've had many different people in it, but I think the people we have now are the best. I'm looking forward to a long run. Catherine, how long are you going to be able to be with us?"

"Oh, I'll be with you as long as Daisy is. She wouldn't go without me."

"Then what do you do that you can go on the road – or are you independently wealthy?"

Chuckling, Catherine replied, "No, I'm not rich, by any means. I'm a financial advisor. I can go anywhere as long as I have my computer. So taking off to be with Daisy is no big deal. It gives me a lot of freedom in my life. So I'm looking forward to traveling with you. I'm also very appreciative that you're letting me."

Jack said, "You're not in the way, and Daisy needs you. So we're glad to have you along."

By this time, the other three had finished eating and were tossing the ball around. So, Gene, Jack, and Catherine got up and got some more to eat. After they were through eating, Gene decided to take a little nap. Jack helped Catherine clean up the picnic area. They put the leftover food in containers for the guys to take with them. They put the tablecloths and dirty dishes in boxes for Catherine to take home. They put the cooler back in the truck and told everyone it was time to go.

Gene got up, helped fold the blanket, and gave it to Daisy. The guys thanked the girls for a great day and wonderful food. The girls got in their car and went to their apartment, while the guys got in the truck and went to their motel. Peter and Tim both thanked the other two for hiring Daisy.

"She's awesome. Things are more fun than before she joined us," said Peter.

Arriving at the motel, they parted ways and each went to their own room to rest for the upcoming week. It was their last week here. Then they would be off to California.

On their way home to their apartment, Daisy talked practically nonstop – about anything and everything. Catherine just smiled at her sister. She had had a good day, too, and was looking forward to the next week.

She had a lot to do before they left to go on the road. But, the biggest thing she had to do was get together with her boss and make sure they had everything worked out perfectly. It was up to her, then, to make sure their plan came together.

CHAPTER 20

ON THE WAY back to the cottage, Wendy stopped at the motel office to see her Aunt Ginny. Ginny was in her usual spot in front of her twelve-inch, black-and-white TV. As soon as she saw Wendy, though, she switched it off, and turned to Wendy with a big smile on her face. She said, "I didn't expect to see you here. How is everything in the cottage? Do you need anything?"

"Everything is fine, Aunt Ginny. It's so comfortable, and we don't need a thing. The reason I'm here is that I wanted to tell you I'm expecting a fax. When you get it, just call me, and I'll run over and pick it up. I don't need to tell you that I don't want anybody to see it."

"I'll let you know as soon as it comes in, Honey."

"Ok, thanks."

Wendy then left the office, blowing her aunt a kiss. Getting back in her car, she was wondering how to tell Dessa and Judy about what happened, without scaring them. She decided that there was no way, so she was just going to tell it the way it was.

When she opened the door and went into the living room, she found the girls huddled over the coffee table. There were papers and a phone book spread all over the table. Not looking up from what they were doing, Judy said, "There's some leftovers in the fridge for you."

"Thanks," she said. "But what are you two doing?

Dessa looked up and answered, "We decided we couldn't let you do all the work, so we've been looking up places where we thought Judy's father's band might have played when they were here. There sure are a lot of them. We put them in categories from ritzy areas to…well…not so ritzy."

"That's really smart thinking. But before we go over that, I need to tell you what happened today." They both looked up at her and sat back on the couch ready to listen. As Wendy told them what had happened, Dessa's mouth dropped open and Judy's face turned a sickly green.

When Wendy was through, Judy exclaimed, "Wendy, I didn't realize how dangerous this was going to be. I can't let either one of you go on with the search. What if something happened to you? Why, I could never forgive myself."

Wendy said to her, "Look, Judy. First of all, this is my job. You two have become my friends, but it's still my job. I feel like we're on the right track, and we must be making someone feel very uncomfortable. Even if you both go home, I'm still going to keep on until I find the answers."

"She's right," said Dessa. "We can't stop now. You would always wonder about your father, and that would drive you nuts. And I've known you long enough, that if you feel that way, you're going to drive ME nuts. So, we go on."

"All right. But, we keep this from our parents. I don't need pressure from them to stop."

"Good. I'm glad you're both in. Now, I don't suppose either one of you can handle a firearm?"

Now, Judy was all smiles. "Dessa is great with a pistol. Her dad taught her, and they used to go practice all the time at the gun club."

"I suppose it's too much to hope that you have a permit to carry," said Wendy.

"My father insisted on it. Sometimes, I had night classes at school and would have to drive home alone late at night. He wanted me to be safe."

Pulling out a 9mm Glock pistol from her purse, she handed it to Dessa, butt first. "Do you think you can handle this?"

"Oh, yeah. I hope I never have to, but, I can hold my own with this."

"Good. Now I'm going to eat those leftovers, and you can show me what you've been doing today."

While Wendy ate, they all went over the lists of places and their locations. They spent a couple of hours going over them and making a plan of action. Having done that, Wendy said, "I don't know about you two, but I'm bushed. Let's get a good night's sleep and hope that picture gets to us early tomorrow, so we can get started."

About ten o'clock the next morning, there was a knock on the door. It was Aunt Ginny with some papers in one hand and a cherry pie in the other, and clean towels over her arm.

Wendy let her in and said, "I'm happy to see the pictures, but that pie is very welcome. I always said that your baking was the best. Thank you so much."

When Aunt Ginny left, with their dirty towels, Dessa took the pie into the kitchen, and Judy took the pictures and studied them intently.

"I have his eyes, don't I?"

Wendy looked at the pictures and said, "Yes, you do. I think he's a pretty good-looking guy, too."

Dessa looked at the pictures and agreed with Wendy.

Judy looked up from the pictures and said, "I think we should get going. I need to find him before my uncle does."

Wendy had a thoughtful look on her face and said, "You know, my Daddy always said that the best defense is a good offense. I have an idea that I think will work. Let me tell you about it."

CHAPTER 21

"WHAT KIND OF idiots did you hire?" Joseph was screaming at Stanley, and then threw his glass at the fireplace, where it smashed into little pieces. Joseph's face was red, and Stanley's was fearful.

When Stanley first came in and told Joseph that Lucille Watkins was still alive and had been whisked away by the police, the room became uncomfortably quiet. After a few minutes, all hell broke loose. That's when Joseph started screaming.

"I was told that they were professionals who knew what they were doing. I guess my sources were wrong," said Stanley.

"That's your trouble. You were guessing. If I were you – and luckily I'm not – I would quit guessing and get somebody who can really do the job. Every day that goes by, they get closer to finding my brother." Going over to Stanley, Joseph spoke in a quiet, but deadly voice. "Stanley, you think I enjoy having this girl killed? Well, I don't. But, I'm not going to share my business with that bastard and his daughter.

Up until now, I've had no problem with him. All he cared about was his music. But, if his daughter finds him, all that could change. He could decide that he needs to impress her, and decide he should share a part of our father's fortune. I..will..never..ever..let..that..happen." As Joseph said the last sentence, he poked a finger in Stanley's chest with every word. Then putting his hands on Stanley's lapels to smooth them out, he said, "Find somebody who can do the job, Stanley. Don't make me have to get a new attorney. Do you understand what I'm saying?"

"Yes…yes, I do."

When Stanley left the room, Joseph went to his phone and punched the button for his assistant. When she answered, he said, "Miss Hensley, call maintenance to come up here right away. I had an accident with my glass, and it needs cleaned up."

When Stanley got into his limo, he immediately placed a call to Vincent. Summoning his sternest voice, he said, "Vincent, you have turned out to be a poor risk. I'm tired of trying to justify your services. Or, should I say, lack of service. You have got to find those girls and eliminate them. And remember. If I go down, so do you. And, if you don't come through – you'll go down anyway."

CHAPTER 22

THE GIRLS GOT in the car with their lists in hand. Dessa had the pistol safely tucked in her purse. She knew she could get to it quickly, if she had to. They were all keeping a sharp lookout for anything or anybody that looked out of place. There was a new look of determination in Judy's eyes.

They spent several hours going in and out of places, showing the pictures, and asking questions.

They got into the car after another no go, and Wendy said, "I think it's time to follow our new plan."

Parking in the same lot as before, they again walked to The Bradburn Pharmaceutical Company offices. Taking the elevator, they were again met by Miss Hensley. "I didn't realize you ladies had an appointment with Mr. Bradburn."

"We don't," said Wendy. "We just wanted to say good-bye to Mr. Bradburn. If we could see him, I promise we won't take up much of his time."

"Have a seat. I'll check with him."

She went back to her desk and picked up the phone. Talking for a minute, she came back to them and said, "Mr. Bradburn said he'd be happy to see you. Please follow me."

She led them to the office, opened the door, and ushered them in, as she had the time before. They went in, and Joseph indicated that they should sit in the chairs in front of his desk.

He said, "It's a pleasure to see you ladies again. I understand you want to say good-bye. Does that mean you have found your father, Miss Winslow?"

"No, I haven't. But, I've spent enough time looking. Dessa and I have to get back home and back to our lives. We're going to stay another couple of days and look over the city. Then we'll be leaving. You were so nice to us the last time we were here, that we just wanted to say thank you and good-bye. If you would get any information on my father, here's my phone number." She handed him a paper with her number on it. "We're sorry we didn't get to meet your father. I'm sure he was a very special man."

"Yes, he was. And, it was nice meeting you ladies. Thank you for stopping to say good-bye to me." He stood up, walked around his desk, and shook their hands. They stood up, and he walked them to the door.

Judy was the last one to walk through the door. As she did, she turned and said, softly, "Good-bye, Uncle Joe." She and the others quickly walked down the hallway and got in the elevator.

The look on Joseph Bradburn's face was one of shock mixed with anger.

When they got in the car, they looked at each other and burst out laughing.

Judy managed to say, "Did you see the look on his face, when I called him Uncle Joe? He couldn't even talk."

"Well, now we're on the same playing level. He knows that we know. Let's get back to work, Ladies," said Wendy.

They went from place to place for hours. They still found nobody that recognized either one of the pictures. Finally, Dessa said, "I can't go on another minute without something to eat. We missed lunch and dinner. We've got to stop and go back to the cottage. We'll get some sleep and start again tomorrow."

Back at the cottage, Wendy said to the girls, "I think I'd better call my office and see if I have any messages. I haven't checked in for a while."

Dialing her number and then her answering machine code, Wendy listened for a few minutes. She got a funny look on her face and hung up the phone. "There was a message from Detective Barlow. He wants us to call him. Maybe he has some information on whoever shot at us."

She got out his card and dialed his number at the station. When he answered on the first ring, she said, "Detective Barlow. This is Wendy Thornberry. I got your message. Do you have some information for us?" She listened to him, then said, "I suppose we could hear you out." She then told him to meet them at a small restaurant close to where they were now. If they had to listen to him, they might as well do it while they were eating.

They pulled into the restaurant parking lot, got out of the car, went in, and found a booth in a quiet corner. There were few people in the place, and the lighting was dim. She had picked a good spot to meet with the detective. They had just ordered when they saw him come in and look around for them. Spotting them, he came over and sat down beside Dessa.

He ordered coffee from the waitress and waited until she was far enough away from them before he spoke. "We want to know why you went to see Joseph Bradburn?"

Wendy, taking the lead, said, "How do you know that, and why should we tell you?"

"We know because we've been watching him for a while. And you should tell us because I think we can help each other get what we want."

Just then the waitress brought their food. After she left and they had picked at their food, Wendy asked, "What is it that you want, Detective?"

"I want to prove that Joseph Bradburn was responsible for his father's death."

Judy gasped and dropped her fork, which landed noisily on her plate. "Why would you think that?"

"We have a connection on the inside. From what this person has told us, we feel it's more than likely that Joseph Bradburn was either directly or indirectly involved in the death of Charles Bradburn. The reason is obvious. He wanted full control over the business. Now, what do you three want?"

Shaken up as she was, Judy still spoke up. "I just found out that Charles Bradburn was my grandfather."

Now it was Detective Barlow's turn to look startled. "Joseph Bradburn is your father?"

"No, he's my uncle. My father is his half-brother. That's why I came here – to find my father." Judy then told the detective the whole story of what they had been going through.

When she had told him everything, he said, "Well, I think you should start calling me Lucas, because I have a feeling we're going to become good friends."

CHAPTER 23

THEY STILL HAD another week in Arizona before they went to California. After they finished the last set on Tuesday night, Jack said that he and Gene needed to talk to everyone. After they had ordered their food, Gene nodded to Jack to go ahead with the meeting.

Jack said, "Gene and I have decided that before we go on to California, we need to change the name of the band. Our name doesn't fit anymore. So we came up with a new one and wanted to know what you have to think about it. The name we came up with is 'Daisy and the Dukes'. What's your opinion?"

Daisy had let out a little squeal when she first heard Jack say the name. "I love it, of course."

Peter and Tim were nodding in agreement. "I can't believe you old guys came up with such a cool name," said Peter, teasing Jack and Gene.

Catherine said, "Well, I guess everyone is in agreement. Even though I don't have a say, I think it's good, too."

"I'm going to call the list of our gigs and tell them about the name change. I think this is a great change to go along with great band members," said Jack.

They all went back to their dinners and Catherine said to Jack and Gene, "This is a really nice thing you are doing. Daisy is going to be even better than ever because of it. Her confidence level isn't very high, so anything that can elevate it, is a good thing. Thanks for doing that."

"If you keep this up, you're going to make me blush," said Gene, grinning at her.

At that, Jack rolled his eyes and grinned, too.

The following afternoon, Jack started calling the places of their upcoming gigs. When the name change was explained, no one had any problem with making the changes on their advertising. For the first time in years, Jack felt like he and Gene were settled. It wasn't that they were going to live in one place like normal people, but they seemed to all be a family. He needed that, and Gene did, too. With Daisy around, Gene seemed to have calmed down a lot. Jack and Gene had been friends for twenty years and were closer than most brothers. Jack was the older brother and knew how to take care of Gene. Suddenly that seemed a little easier to do.

The rest of the week went by in a flash. When the guys were getting packed up to leave, Catherine and Daisy pulled up in their car. They were all ready. As they pulled up, Jack told them that he had talked to the owner of the next place they were headed.

"Here's what Mel told me: 'Jack, I've got bad news for you. We had a fire and won't be back up and running for a couple of weeks. I've got an alternative for you, though. A friend of mine runs a place in San Francisco, and he could use your band for the two weeks that you're missing here. How about it? I know it's a longer drive, but he said for you to take your time and start whenever you got there. Do you want the job?'

"I told him we'd be glad to take it. He gave me the information, and I told him we would be there as soon as possible. I'm glad he got a hold of me. Two weeks without work would not be good for us.

"He said he'd call us in San Francisco when he was ready for us."

As Jack gave everyone the new directions, he got an eerie feeling. Shrugging it off, he got in his truck and they were on their way.

CHAPTER 24

L UCAS PICKED THE girls up the next afternoon so they could take some more names off their lists. Wendy said, "Lucas, we decided that you should drive us around and we'll go into the places with the pictures. You look too much like a cop, and we don't think we'll get very far with you by our side."

He was tall, dark, and handsome with gorgeous gray eyes. He dressed well, maybe a little too well. If he hadn't become a cop, he could have been a model. He just had the attitude and stature that said "cop".

It took them two more days, but they finally found the right person. Her name was Eunice and she was the bartender and owner of Eunice's Bar. Eunice looked to be in her late fifties. She looked more like someone's granny than a bar owner. The Bar was dark and old, but the people there looked to be having a good time. The girls sat down at the bar and ordered lemonades. When Eunice served them, Judy asked, "I'm looking for my father, and I have two pictures of him. One was when he was in his early twenties, and one is what he might look like now. Would you look at them and see if you recognize him? He's in a band and might have played here."

"Sure, honey. Let me see those pictures." Taking them and going over to where there was better lighting, Eunice studied them for several minutes. Then she closed her eyes and put her finger to her chin as if she was going back over the years in her mind, like you would run a microfilm machine. Finally, she got a pleased look on her face. Coming back over to the bar, she said, "I believe I know who he is. His band has been here two or three times. The first time was about twenty years ago and the second time about eight years ago. I believe he was here about six months ago, too."

Wendy asked her, "Do you remember the name of the band? That would go a long way to helping us find him. You don't know how much this means to us."

"I think I can, just by the look on this little one's face. Now let me think a minute. Noreen. Come here and help me with something."

Noreen was a pretty, petite, redhead, with a sunny smile. She looked like her disposition brought her a lot of tips. When she got to the bar and greeted the girls, Eunice handed her the updated picture and said, "This gentleman was in a band that was here about six months ago. Do you remember the name of the band?"

Noreen also studied the picture she was handed. "Yes, Eunice. I do think I remember. Wasn't it Aces and Eights?"

"Of course, that was the name."

Judy said, excitedly, "That's wonderful! Thanks to both of you. You don't happen to know where they might have gone from here, do you?"

They both shook their heads no, but Eunice said, "Why don't you try the diner across the street? I think the fellows went over there to eat after they got done here. Vickie might have heard something. I'm sure she would tell you if she did."

After thanking Eunice and Noreen, the girls stopped at the car and told Lucas what was going on.

"I knew if we just kept hunting, we'd find out something. Since the diner is the next stop, let's all go in and get something to eat. We haven't eaten all day."

So they all went into the diner. Again, luck was on their side. Their waitress had a name tag on that said 'Vickie'.

When they placed their orders, Lucas asked Vickie, "It doesn't look like you're too busy in here tonight. Could you come back here when you put our orders in? Eunice said you might be able to help us with something."

"Sure thing. Be happy to help." She went to the kitchen window and placed their orders, then came right back with the drinks for them and a cup of coffee for herself. "Now what can I do for you?"

Once more, Judy got out the pictures and showed them to Vickie. She explained about her father and what Eunice had told them.

After Vickie looked them over, she said, "Eunice is right. It was about six months ago that they were in here. Great guys and good tippers."

"Did they mention where they might be going after they left here?"

"As a matter of fact, they did. It was Rome. I only remember it because I laughed and asked them if they meant Italy or Georgia." They all laughed at that. By that time, their orders were ready. Vickie got up and went to get them. She left them alone after they were served.

Dessa said, "I guess we're on our way to Rome, Georgia, aren't we?"

"Yes, and I'm right there with you," said Lucas. "The boss said I'm to go all the way with you."

"Let's eat up, get some rest, and we'll leave first thing in the morning," said Wendy.

When Dessa and Judy got into their beds and had turned out the lights, Judy said, "I talked to my parents when you were getting ready for bed."

"You did? How are they?"

"My father sounded all right, but my mother sounded fakey. You know, like when a person is trying to be cheerful, but they really aren't. Dessa, am I doing the right thing? I want to find my biological father, but I don't want to make things any harder on my mother."

"Judy, your mother is stronger than you give her credit for. She just misses you, that's all. I think in her own way, she's proud of you for going after something that's important to you. We've come this far. Let's see it to the end. I think you owe it to, not only yourself, but to your father and your grandfather."

Judy was silent for several seconds and then she said, softly, "You're right, Dessa. Thanks for being there with me on this. You are my best friend, and I love you."

"That's what best friends do for one another. I love you, too. Now let's get some sleep. Tomorrow morning will be here in no time."

CHAPTER 25

THE BAND GOT into San Francisco a couple of days early. They checked into their motel, which was a little bit above what they were used to. Mel had told Jack that he would make the reservations for them and foot the bill, since he felt bad about the trouble he had caused them.

Jack, Gene, Catherine, and Daisy decided to do the tourist thing. They wanted to see as much of San Francisco as they could in the two days they had off. Peter and Tim, as usual, wanted to go scope out the girls.

San Francisco was an exciting city. They took a cable car to the top of Lombard Street and walked down the crooked block. The flowers lining the sides of the street were beautiful and very colorful. They had each bought a throw-away camera, so they were taking pictures everywhere, the goofier, the better.

They took the ferry to Alcatraz and used the self-guided audio tour to find out about the different places within the former prison. The tour also told them about some of the famous (or infamous, depending on how you looked at it) prisoners who had lived there. They were just like most tourists and wanted to see the cell that housed Al Capone.

One of the most beautiful parks in the country was the Golden Gate Park. Stopping at a small grocery store, they got luncheon items and decided to have a late lunch in the park.

After they had finished their lunch, Gene said, "This sightseeing is wearing me out. I could take a nap right about now."

"Gene, you could take a nap about any time," laughed Jack. "Why don't we look around the park a while, and then we can go back to the motel. We can see the bridge from there. I'd like to watch the sun set through the bridge. What about all of you?"

They all agreed with him. So they continued to look through the park at the Dutch windmills and the remote-controlled boats. Kids of all ages had a boat in the water. There was a set of twins who were squealing with delight. They even saw a herd of buffalo. The buffalo didn't seem too excited to see people watching them. Other than an occasional snort or two, they just kept grazing.

Then they grabbed a cab and went back to the motel. When they got there, they found chairs outside by the pool. They had been lucky all day. No fog. Their luck continued as they sipped cocktails and talked about their day. As the sun started to drop into the ocean, conversation stopped as they enjoyed the breathtaking sight. The colors were magnificent. The reds, yellows, blues, and purples were a sight to behold.

Finally, Gene said, "As much fun as this has been, folks, I'm beat. I'm going to get plenty of sleep tonight."

"I'm going to watch some TV and maybe read a little bit," said Daisy. "Come on, Gene. I'll walk you home." She leaned down and gave her sister a hug and kiss.

"Ok. Good night, people," said Gene.

"Back at cha, partner," replied Jack.

After Daisy and Gene went inside, Jack got two more drinks and then sat back down. "So, Catherine, how are you liking the journey so far?"

"I'm loving it, but, I have a feeling that today isn't a normal day for all of you."

"No, it certainly isn't. Maybe you and Daisy are bringing us good luck. What would you like to do tomorrow?"

"I'd like to go to Chinatown and Fisherman's Wharf. I understand you can't come to San Francisco and not go to those places. The tour book says that Chinatown in San Francisco is not only the largest outside of Asia but, also, the oldest in North America. Fisherman's

Wharf has a Sea Lion Center, Giradelli Square, and Madame Tussands.

Wharf has a Sea Lion Center, Giradelli Square, and Madame Tussands. I think it would probably take a week to see these two places."

"Well, since we only have tomorrow, we'd better get some sleep and start out early."

"I think you're right."

Jack walked Catherine to her room and then went on to his. He climbed into his bed and went to sleep as soon as his head sank into the pillow. He was so tired from the day of sightseeing, that he slept, dreamless, until the alarm woke him at eight o'clock. He called Gene to make sure he was up and then went to take his shower.

The four amigos (as Daisy called them) all met at the motel's restaurant for breakfast at eight thirty and then left for Fisherman's Wharf. They saw the adorable sea lions on Pier 39. The guys made faces at them and the seals barked back. When they went to Madame Tussauds, they had to pose with the figures, just like any other tourist. The girls gravitated to George Clooney, while the guys decided to pose with Madonna.

Gene said, "I wonder if Madonna looks better in wax or in the flesh? Someone is a really good artist to be able to make copies of people that look so good."

After that, they decided to hit Ghiradelli Square for hot fudge sundaes. They also bought some chocolate chip cookies for a late night snack and to give Peter and Tim.

While eating their sundaes, Daisy said, "It says here on the menu that Ghiradelli's is the oldest, continuously operating chocolate maker in the country. It also says that Mr. Ghiradelli came here during the gold rush and opened a store. The miners needed things to spend their gold dust on, so he started selling them chocolates. Wow! I know how much I love chocolate. I just didn't know how much people were willing to spend for it."

Full of ice cream and chocolate, the next stop was Chinatown. It was an amazing place. They browsed some of the small shops, tasted some of the wonderful food, and looked at the buildings that denoted the beautiful architecture of the Chinese. Later in the day, they decided to eat before they went back to the motel. They found a quaint little hole-in-the-wall place to eat. The food was delicious, the service great, and the people were very friendly. They went back to the motel full and happy from a wonderful day.

They grabbed some beers and, again, sat by the pool to watch the sun set. Then, they all headed off to bed for much-needed sleep.

CHAPTER 26

THE THREE WOMEN and Lucas started early on their almost eleven-hour drive to Rome, Georgia. The plan was for them to change drivers often, so that they could drive straight through. No one wanted breakfast so early, but they did each have a mug of coffee. The two who were in the back would take a nap, while the passenger in the front seat would keep the driver awake. This was working out quite well.

The only problem, unknown to the four, was the two men in the black sedan following them at a discrete distance. They kept pace with the women and Lucas and went completely unobserved.

By the time they reached Georgia, Wendy said, "I think we should go ahead and get a motel. One more day isn't going to make a difference, and we all need a good night's sleep." The others agreed with her.

They found a place that looked reasonable on the outside. Lucas went in to register for their rooms. The black sedan stayed in the shadows, and when Lucas drove them around to their rooms, the men went in to register, and requested rooms on the opposite side. They took turns hiding in the shadows, throughout the night, to make sure they kept track of their prey.

The women had decided to share a room, while Lucas, of course, had his own. While Dessa and Judy were getting ready for bed, Wendy said, "I think I'm going to go outside and get a breath of fresh air. I think it will help me get to sleep. I'm a little keyed up after the drive up here." She then stepped outside and sat in one of the chairs that were scattered about the porch of the motel. Shortly, Lucas came out of his room. Looking around, he noticed Wendy and came over to her.

"I guess we both had the same idea," he said, sitting in the chair next to her. "Are you getting some air, too?"

"Yes, plus I need to quiet my mind. I always seem to do more thinking when I'm trying to get to sleep," she answered.

"I seem to have that problem, too. So, what are your thoughts tonight?" he asked.

"I think that we need to find Judy's father soon. I don't know how much more of this stress she can take. She's trying to act tough, but she's not, and it's beginning to show. Dessa is the only thing keeping Judy going. What's on your mind?" she asked.

"I've noticed the same thing. If someone came up behind her and said 'boo', I think she would actually jump six feet in the air."

Laughing at the image of that, Wendy said, "I couldn't have put it any better than that."

They continued to sit there for a few minutes longer.

Lucas asked, "Wendy, why did you become a private detective?"

"My father left me the business," she replied.

"Wait a minute. Was your father, Mitchell Thornberry?"

"Yes, he was." Her voice had a sad tone to it when she said that.

"I didn't know him, but I have certainly heard of him. He was a good cop."

"Yes, he was. When he retired, he went private. He taught me everything I needed to know. I worked with him for a while before he died. I couldn't think of anything I wanted to do more than be a private investigator. Quid pro quo. Why did you become a cop?"

Lucas looked thoughtful. Then he said, "I wanted to make a difference. Now, wait. I know that sounds corny, but it's the truth. I thought I could help people and make their lives better. Sometimes, it does. Most of the time, not so much."

They sat there, quietly, for a few minutes more.

Finally, Wendy got up and said, "I guess I should try to get some sleep now. We'll see you in the morning, Lucas. We're just going to sleep until we wake up on our own. I think everybody needs that."

Lucas replied, "I agree. I'm going in now, too. Good night."

They both went in to their respective rooms and immediately went to sleep.

They all slept in the next morning, but Dessa was the first one up. She quietly got her clothes and went into the bathroom to get ready for the day. After showering and dressing, she went out into the bedroom, where she found Judy and Wendy awake. Judy was talking to her mother and Wendy was intently studying the phone book.

"How are your parents, Judy?" asked Dessa.

"Mother tries to put on a good front, but I can tell she really misses me. Father just says things to keep me going. He said he's taking good care of Mother and for us to keep going. He said to tell you that your mom and dad said hello and wish us well. Dessa, I'm so grateful that they are ok with you being here with me. I couldn't do this without you."

"Then it's a good thing you don't have to," replied Dessa. "Wendy, do you have a list of places to search today?"

"Yes, I do. Let's finish getting ready, and then we can get something to eat. After that, we'll be ready to start hunting. Judy, you can go ahead in the bathroom, and I'll call Lucas to let him know of our plans."

They got ready to go and met Lucas outside. They stopped at a local diner and got a hearty meal. Then, with list in hand, they started on their search. They continued as they had in Miami. The only difference was that they had company everywhere they went.

Having the band name this time made things go a lot faster. Late that evening they came across the bar where the Aces and Eights band had played. The owner of the bar, Millie, sat down with them at their table. When it was explained to her why they were looking for the band, she smiled and relaxed.

"I know one of the places that these guys were going to be playing," said Millie. "They were going to be in Goodyear, Arizona. My cousin, Bubba, is the bartender at The Beer Keg. I called him and let him know how well-liked they were here. He talked to Jack and made arrangements for the band to play there. I don't know what the dates were for their gig, but I can call my cousin and you can talk to him."

Wendy said, "That would be a tremendous help, Millie. Can we call him now?"

"Of course. Let's go into my office, and we'll get him on the phone. I'll send another round of drinks over while you're waiting. On me."

The others all said, "Thank you."

When Wendy and Millie went to Millie's office, Judy grabbed Dessa's hand and exclaimed, "Oh, Dessa. I think this is the best lead we've had since we started. We're finally getting close."

"Yes, Judy, we are. But, I think if we're going to go to Arizona, we need to switch to flying instead of driving. That will get us there so much faster. Don't you agree, Lucas?"

"That sounds like the best way to go. If we drove, it would take too long, and we could lose them. We've got to catch up with them," said Lucas. "Let's wait until Wendy comes back before we make too many plans."

Wendy and Millie came back just then – Wendy with a big grin on her face. "Ladies and gentleman, we're going to Arizona. Judy, your dad has been there recently, and I was told by Bubba that we aren't far behind them."

When they left, everyone thanked Millie and shook her hand. Judy added a huge smile and hug to go along with her thanks.

CHAPTER 27

A S MISS HENSLEY showed the attorney into the office, she heard Joseph Bradburn say, "Welcome, Stanley. Come in and pour us both a drink."

With a surprised look on his face, Stanley went to the bar and poured them each a healthy amount of Scotch. He handed a glass to Joseph and they both sat down.

After taking a drink, Joseph said, "Stanley, I've decided to let you off the hook. I've got a handle on the situation with my brother. I've taken on someone I know and can trust. I've given him carte blanche to hire whoever he needs and spend whatever is needed to take care of the situation. In fact, I have information that everyone has gone to Arizona."

"Arizona? Why Arizona?" asked Stanley.

"Because after the girls went to Georgia, they went to Arizona. You see, I didn't believe for one minute that they had given up looking for my brother. And they hadn't. So Arizona is the next stop. I must admit, that following them and letting them do all the work, isn't so bad. We are getting close, Stanley.

"I realized that you were out of your element in this situation. Now you can go back to being just my attorney. Of course, you must remember that you are an accessory to anything that happens. But, who am I to tell you, the lawyer, the law? Now, let's have another drink and order in a nice lunch."

CHAPTER 28

L ANDING IN ARIZONA, the four went to rent a car to take them into Goodyear. They went immediately to see Millie's cousin, Bubba. When they walked into the bar, the man behind the counter gave them a wide grin.

He said, "You must be the people Millie told me about. Welcome. Which one of you is Wendy?"

"That would be me," said Wendy, as she walked over to shake Bubba's hand. "We're very glad to meet you."

"Can I get you something to drink?" offered Bubba.

"Thanks for the hospitality," said Lucas, "but time is of the essence. Can you tell us where Aces and Eights was going next?"

"They said they were headed to L. A. I believe it was a club they have played at before. I was trying to think of the name of it. I think the name of it is The Dusty Rose."

Judy repeated, "The Dusty Rose. It sounds wonderful to have a name. Let's leave right now."

Dessa asked, "Bubba, about how long does it take to get to Los Angeles?"

"Well, if you're driving, it's about five or six hours, depending on the traffic."

"Wouldn't it be better to fly there?" asked Judy.

Wendy said, "I'm not sure it would be any faster, Judy. By the time we go back to the airport, get a plane, fly to L. A., then rent another car, and get to the club, I don't think it would be any faster than just taking off now and driving there."

"I'm in agreement with Wendy," said Dessa. "I know you're excited, Judy, but I think that since we already have the van, we should just drive there."

"I guess you're right. Why don't we get some sandwiches and coffee to take with us?"

Bubba spoke up, "I'll fix up a nice basket of food for you to take along. You just go sit down, and I'll get busy."

"We've got a couple of Thermos bottles in the van. I'll go get them, Bubba, and you can just fill them up," volunteered Lucas. "I'll be right back."

The girls sat down at a table, and Lucas went out to get the Thermos bottles. When he came back in, he had a strange look on his face. After giving them to Bubba, he sat down at the table with them.

"I hate to tell you this, but we have a problem," he said to them.

When all eyes were on him, he continued. "All our tires are slashed."

Judy gasped. Dessa said "What?" But Wendy just stared at him with a look of disbelief.

Finally Wendy said, "Do you think this was a neighborhood gang who did this, Lucas?"

Hesitating for a moment, he said, "No, I don't. When we were in Georgia, I thought I spotted two men following us. But, I wasn't sure. I didn't say anything, because I thought I was just imagining it. I only saw them that one time, and I haven't seen them since we got here. Now, I'm wondering if they caught up with us."

Dessa said, "What are we going to do now?"

"We need to get the van fixed before we can do anything else," said Wendy.

Lucas spoke up, "Judy, let's go talk to Bubba and see what he can do to help us. Dessa, you and Wendy stay here and try to come up with a plan for our next move."

Lucas and Judy went to Bubba at the bar and told him what had happened. They didn't let on that it was anything other than kids who had done the dirty deed.

Bubba said, "One of my waitresses has a brother who's a mechanic.

I'm sure he can get the tires you need and come here to put them on for you. You should call the police and let them know what happened."

"I don't think we'll bother with the police," said Lucas. "They won't be able to do anything about it, and it will just slow us down even more than ever."

"Lucas is right," said Judy. "Can you call your waitress and make the arrangements for us, please? Tell her we'll pay cash. And we'd appreciate it, the sooner the better."

"Sure. I'll call her right now." They waited while Bubba made the phone call. He was back in just a few minutes. "Maria will call her brother and tell him to get right over here to check out your van. Why don't you all wait at the table and I'll bring some food over to you. I'll keep the lunch I made for you, and you can still take that with you."

After Bubba served them burgers and fries, Wendy spoke up, "Dessa and I were talking about what we should do now. It's going to take a while to put new tires on the van, so we think we should find a motel and get some sleep. We can start off fresh in the morning. As for the men following us, we'll just have to keep a better eye out for them. And, Lucas, don't hide anything like that from us again, please. We all need to be aware of what's going on."

"You're right, Wendy. I'm sorry about that."

CHAPTER 29

THE FIRST WEEK they played in San Francisco went by in a flash. The people loved them, and they played to a full house every night. Catherine always sat at a small table set up where she could see the band, and they could see her. She had her laptop on the table, and that's when she got the work done that she needed to do for her job. The band was playing better than ever. When Daisy came along, everyone seemed to play with a lot more pep. Playing before had started to be work. Now the fun was back in it. Jack and Gene felt younger than they had in years.

When they weren't playing at the club, the four of them were out exploring the city and going back to places they found that they really loved. Peter and Tim, as usual, went where the younger crowd hung out.

Where Jack and Gene had usually eaten at diners, they and the girls now found quaint, little, off-the-beaten-track places. They walked a lot to keep the pounds off. None of them wanted any of those extras.

They also made good use of the motel pool. The weather was perfect for swimming and lounging around. The water in the pool was always the right temperature for them. It seemed like the times that were available to them for the pool wasn't a popular time for others, so it was easy to feel like the pool belonged to them.

One day, while at the pool, Daisy and Gene were swimming and tossing a beach ball to each other. Jack and Catherine were having a quiet conversation.

Jack summoned up enough courage to ask Catherine, "Are you really going to stay with us as long as Daisy is playing?"

Catherine thought a while before answering. "That's my intention. I guess it all depends on my job. After all, I do have an obligation to my employer. So far, everything has been working out well. I don't have any reason to believe otherwise. But, that could always change, of course."

"I hope it doesn't," he said, quietly. "I like having you around. I know Gene is having more fun than ever, with Daisy around. I'm getting rather attached to you, too. I've almost forgotten what it was like when the two of you weren't around. I sure don't want to go back to the old way, either. Besides, then we'd have to change our name again."

They both laughed at that. Then, suddenly, Jack leaned toward Catherine and gave her a gentle kiss on the lips. She looked surprised but didn't pull away from him. From then on, they would sneak quick kisses when no one was looking. They felt like teenagers again.

Although they were certainly old enough to take things "to the next level" as the saying goes, they were in no hurry. It would have been easy enough, since Jack and Gene always had separate rooms, but both Jack and Catherine were content with the magic moments. Neither were ready for anything more – at least, not for the time being.

One day, while the girls were off on a shopping spree, Jack and Gene found themselves alone at the pool. Gene asked Jack, "What do you think about Daisy?"

"I think she's a great bass player, and she adds a lot to the band," replied Jack.

Looking slightly miffed, Gene said, "No, that's not what I mean. Do you think I would be crazy to fall for her?"

"Oh, that. No, I don't think so. She's a little wacky, but in a good way. I think you two seem to fit pretty good together. And, besides, I'm falling for her sister. So it's kind of a good thing that you *are* falling for Daisy. After all, we're best friends. Works out pretty good, don't you think?" replied Jack.

"Yeah, it does." With that, they clinked their beer bottles together, sighed, and sat back to enjoy the rest of their lazy afternoon.

That night was a very happy one for everyone. Jack and Gene couldn't keep the smiles off their faces. They only had a few more days before they went to Los Angeles for their next gig. Mel had come through for them in a big way. Not only had he gotten this opportunity for them in San Francisco along with a great motel, but he had promised them an additional week at his club. Life was looking pretty good for them right now.

CHAPTER 30

"SO HOW CLOSE do you think you are to my baby brother?" asked Joseph.

The voice on the other end answered, "Not sure, but we're heading towards L. A. There's been a complication."

"Oh, what kind of complication?"

"It seems that someone slashed all four tires on their van," said the voice.

"Well, that does slow things down a little, doesn't it?" asked Joseph. He didn't really expect an answer to this. But his obvious sarcasm went right over the head of his co-conspirator.

"For a day, anyway, Boss."

"Well, the longer it takes for my niece and her friends to look for that band, the more of a chance there is that they have moved on. I don't care if they are following them all over this country for the next year. The longer it takes, maybe they'll eventually give up. Then my company will be safely in my hands and my hands alone. So get back to work."

CHAPTER 31

AFTER SPENDING A restless night, Lucas and the women got up to find the van parked outside. Not only did it have new tires, but it was washed and had the gas tank filled.

Judy said to the others, "Why don't we leave now and stop later for something to eat. I really want to get to L. A., and I'm not very hungry right now."

The others agreed with her, and they piled in the car with Lucas in the driver's seat. They drove for about three hours in silence.

Then Lucas spoke up, "Let's stop at the next place where I can top off the tank before we get to Los Angeles. We can get something to eat, too. I'm getting hungry. I could use a burger and fries. How about it, Ladies?"

The others agreed, and he stopped at the next restaurant he came to that had a gas station. While he gassed up the van, the others went inside the diner and ordered. They all got burgers and fries, which turned out to be very tasty. Judy was the only one who didn't seem to be hungry.

When they had finished, and Judy paid the check, they got on their way again to L. A. They drove mostly in silence except for checking the directions. When they got into the city, they went directly to the club. It was early, so it didn't seem strange to have only a few cars in the parking lot.

They parked outside the main entrance, and Wendy said, "Here we are. Hopefully, this is the end of our search. Let's go inside and see."

They all got out of the car, with Judy bringing up the rear. She had been quiet all day and was very pale, too.

When they opened the door and walked in, the beauty of the interior was striking. As the name of the club suggested, "The Dusty Rose," the wall coloring was various shades of that color, graduating from a darker shade at the bottom to a lighter shade near the ceiling. The carpeting was a beautiful shade of dusty blue, and there were green plants everywhere. It was quite stunning. There was a large stage where bands would set up, and the dance floor seemed to be large enough to hold a hundred people.

For a few moments, all they could do was look around and admire the beauty of the place. Just when they decided to find someone to talk to, a man dressed in khakis, an open collar shirt, and loafers came out of an office down the hall.

Seeing that he had company, the man walked up to them, smiled, and introduced himself to them. "I'm Mel Hoverman. I own The Dusty Rose. How may I help you?"

Wendy spoke up, "Mr. Hoverman, I'm Wendy Thornberry, a private investigator from Miami, Florida. These are associates of mine. We're looking for a band called Aces and Eights. We were told they were playing here."

"It's a pleasure to meet you all. I believe the band you are talking about has changed its name to 'Daisy and the Dukes'. And, yes, they are supposed to be here for three weeks. However, we've been closed for repairs, and I got them a job in San Francisco. They won't be playing here until tomorrow night. In fact, I'm not even sure they're in town yet. Is there something I can do for you?"

"No there isn't, Mr. Hoverman. I guess we'll just have to wait until tomorrow," said Dessa. "What time do you think they will be here to set up?"

"I imagine they'll come in sometime after noon. They'll want to get their gear set up and do sound checks. You're welcome to come in then. Is there any message I can give them when they show up?"

"No," said Wendy, "but, we'll be back tomorrow around one. Thank you for your kindness. I'm sure we'll see you then."

"I'll be here."

Back in the van, they all had a look of disappointment on their faces. Judy broke the silence and said, "I guess we'd better find a motel. I'm beginning to wonder if I'm ever going to find my father."

CHAPTER 32

THEY FOUND A nice hotel and decided to order from room service. They had gotten a three-bedroom suite. Judy had decided that they needed to rest in a calming atmosphere tonight. Besides the bedrooms, each with an attached bath, there was a central living room. Wendy had her own room, Lucas, naturally, had his own, and Dessa and Judy shared the third room.

Rooms like this usually had modern furniture that seemed cold. But this room had beautiful tables of cherry wood, overstuffed chairs and couches in a golden, brocade fabric. The walls were covered in a pale green linen-like wallpaper, and there were touches of greenery everywhere. There was even a fireplace, which was more for decoration than usefulness. But it was there for those rare occasions when it might be needed.

The bedrooms were decorated in equally elegant cherry furniture and brocaded chairs in shades of red, blue, and gold. The bathrooms were a woman's delight. There was a soaking tub and separate shower in each one. The towels were bright white, soft, and thick. Of course, there was the obligatory robes with matching slippers.

They all took a quick shower to wash off the dust of the road, so to speak, while they were waiting on room service to bring them steak dinners. They had opened the bottle of champagne that the management had waiting in their room when they got there. Management had also sent up a lovely arrangement of various colored roses and a basket of fruit, which they were going to have for dessert.

All-in-all the suite was fit for a king – or rather, a king and three queens.

After they had enjoyed the delicious dinner, the strain of the last few days seemed to set in, so they all decided to get some sleep. They all looked and felt done in, but the stress was very apparent on Judy's face.

When she and Dessa went into their room, Dessa asked, "Judy, are you ok? You look pretty pale. I'm concerned about you."

"I'm fine, Dessa," Judy answered. "I just need a good night's sleep. Tomorrow I get to meet my father. Then this whole thing will be over, and you and I can go back to our normal lives again." She got into bed, turned on her side, and closed her eyes.

Dessa sighed and did the same.

Something awakened her. Dessa opened her eyes and looked at the clock on the table beside the bed. It was three thirty in the morning. Turning over, she saw that Judy was gone. That must have been what had awakened her. Noticing that the bathroom door was open and the light was off, she went to the door to the living room and opened it. Looking out, she saw Judy sitting on the couch with a cup and saucer in her hands. Walking quietly so as not to disturb anyone else, she went over and sat down beside her. She saw a tea service sitting on the coffee table with extra cups and saucers, so she poured herself a cup of the sweet-smelling tea.

"Why are you sitting here having a tea party without me?" she asked Judy.

"I'm sorry if I woke you up, Dessa. I was so tired, but I just couldn't sleep. So I ordered some herbal tea from room service. With as much tea and all the extra cookies and tea sandwiches they sent, you would think I was having a party. I was trying to be quiet."

The look on Judy's face was so sorrowful and childlike, that it made Dessa want to cry. She said, "Oh, Judy, you should have gotten me up. We're best friends, and I feel awful that you were sitting out here all by yourself. Are you just too excited to sleep?"

"I don't know, Dessa. I get excited. Then I get panicky. Then I get scared. I don't know what to expect. His letters seem to say that he loves me, but what if he just wrote those things, because he never expected to ever meet me. He may not really want to have me in his life. And, what if I don't like him. He may be a real creep. Then this adventure has all been for nothing. I would have spent Alexander's money and hurt him and my mother for my selfishness."

"First of all, if Alexander didn't want you to spend the money, he wouldn't have offered it to you. He and your mother are behind this search one hundred percent. What if all the other things are true? Wouldn't you rather know if your father is a creep than to always wonder if he is? I'll admit that, at first, I was a little concerned about this whole thing, but as we went on, I decided that it was the best thing for you to do. Don't give up yet."

There was silence for a while as they sat there drinking their tea. Putting her cup down, Judy finally turned to Dessa and said, "Thank you. You're right. I can't give up now. What a waste that would be. I think I can sleep now. Dessa, you've always been my best friend. I don't know what I would do without you."

"I don't plan on you ever having to find out, either. Let's get some sleep. We've got a big day tomorrow."

They got up and went into their room. In just a few minutes, they were both sound asleep.

CHAPTER 33

W HEN SHE GOT up the next morning, Wendy saw the tea service sitting on the coffee table. Noticing that two cups had been used, she figured out that Judy and Dessa must have had a rough night. So she wasn't surprised when they didn't come out of their room until almost noon.

Lucas had joined her, fresh from the shower, at about nine. She showed him the set and told him her theory. Turning on the TV and keeping the volume low, so as not to disturb the other two, Wendy said, "Judy really needed her sleep. After all, today is the day she has been waiting for during this whole search."

When Dessa and Judy came out of their room, Judy said, "We're ready to go. Let's get on the way."

Wendy asked, "Are you ok today, Judy? It appears you might have been up late last night?"

"Thanks for being concerned, Wendy. Yes, I was. But, thanks to Dessa, I'm just fine today. I'm anxious to get going."

They went down to the car, with Judy and Dessa in the back, Wendy and Lucas in the front, with Lucas driving. They drove the short distance to the club, and parked near some vehicles that hadn't been there the day before.

Getting out of the car, Lucas took Judy's arm and squeezed it with reassurance. He said, "Everything's going to be all right, Judy."

"I know it is, Lucas. Thanks for helping us. I owe you a lot."

"You don't owe me anything. Don't forget, I'm looking for information, too. Come on. Let's go inside."

They followed Wendy and Dessa into the club. It was dim inside, and it took them a moment to adjust their eyes. As they walked from the entryway into the club area, they saw tables set up for the evening. At a table near the stage, there was a man and woman drinking cups of coffee and immersed in conversation. On the stage was the band equipment, being set up by three men and a woman. While the club was dimly lit, the stage was bathed in bright lights.

Judy's eyes went immediately to the man on stage, who with the woman, was setting up the drums. "That's him. My dad. He looks just like the picture we have."

Before she had a chance to say anything else, Lucas grabbed her and held her tightly in front of him. He had a gun against her temple. She screamed! All eyes turned toward them. Wendy went for her gun, the people at the table jumped up, equipment was dropped on stage.

"Don't anybody do anything stupid!" Lucas' voice was harsh. His whole attitude had changed in an instant. "Miss Thornberry, slowly put the gun on the floor and kick it over here." She complied, reluctantly. "Now your clutch piece, too. That goes for your gun, too, Miss Stanton. Do not underestimate me. I will shoot her if I have to." She, also, did as she was told.

"I only want Judy and her dad. Believe me, this is nothing personal. It's just a job."

Wendy attempted to keep Lucas talking. "Who's paying you for this job? Joseph Bradburn?"

"How clever of you to realize that, Wendy. Yes, he is."

"And there weren't two men after us, were there? You slashed our tires," said Dessa, picking up on what Wendy was trying to do.

"Well, Dessa, you're half right. I did slash the tires. But there were two men after us. I think we lost them. I don't know who they were, but I'm assuming they were the 'good guys'. Now enough of this chit chat. You know all you need to know. I want you two at the table, and Wendy and Dessa, to stand closer to the stage. You people on the stage come toward the front of it. You, Daddy, stay where you are. I'm going to take care of you right now. Then, Judy comes with me."

As he started to point the gun at Gene, all hell broke loose. Judy saw her chance, and stomped her foot down on Lucas'. Daisy pushed Gene out of the way. He fell backward over his drums. Daisy and Catherine both pulled guns out of holsters wrapped around their legs. Lucas' gun went off and hit Dessa in the arm. Judy dropped to the floor. Lucas wasn't sure who to go after, so he just waved his gun around. When he went to shoot again, he was hit by the bullets from the guns of Daisy and Catherine.

As he dropped to the floor in a pool of blood, the women ran toward him. Suddenly two men came running in from the front door with guns drawn.

Detective Jacoby immediately ran over to Lucas and knelt down beside the dying man. "Why, Lucas? Why did you do this?"

Gasping for air, Lucas answered him, "I needed the money, Jake. Joseph Bradburn was going to pay me a lot of it. I'm sorry I let you down. I never wanted you to find out." That was all he could manage to say before he slid into death.

Detective Jacoby laid him, gently, on the floor and looked up to find the others standing in a group a discreet distance away from them. He stood and said to the man with him, "Officer Swenson, please call this in to the local precinct."

Catherine and Daisy came up to Detective Jacoby. They had holstered their guns. They spoke quietly to him. Nodding, he then walked over to the others.

Just then, a voice came from the stage. "Hey, what's going on out there? I could use a little help here. I think my leg is broken."

Daisy started running up to Gene, yelling over her shoulder for someone to call an ambulance. Judy ran after her. As she reached her father, Judy touched him, gently, on the shoulder. They stared at each other, emotions going through their minds. Finally, Judy said, "Hi, Dad. It's good to see you."

"You're as beautiful as I had imagined," he told her.

That's all the conversation that was possible, because the paramedics were there trying to get Gene on the gurney to put him in the ambulance. Judy and Daisy went with him.

Wendy and Jack were both helping Dessa. They had made her

sit down at a table, before she fell down from shock. Wendy always carried a small first aid kit with her, and she found some gauze. Jack was wrapping it around her wound and had taken a large handkerchief from his pocket to make a sling.

He said, "It's just a flesh wound. I'm sure it hurts, but it should heal up just fine."

"It's ok. I had a tetanus shot once that hurt worse. Is everyone else all right?" she asked.

"I think I heard Gene say something about a broken leg, but everyone else looks all right," said Jack.

The police had come into the club with the paramedics. Detective Jacoby showed his badge to the officer who seemed to be in charge.

There was just as much action now as there had been a minutes before – only without the bullets.

CHAPTER 34

THEY WERE STANDING around Gene's hospital bed talking and laughing. Judy and Daisy were each holding one of his hands. Jack and Catherine were there, along with Wendy and Dessa, who had her arm in a hospital sling. Tim and Peter had been there earlier, but had gone out to look for a temporary, substitute drummer.

"If it wasn't so inconvenient, a guy could get used to all this attention," said Gene, as he looked lovingly first at his daughter and then at Daisy.

"Yeah, well, don't get used to it. As soon as that leg heals, you'd better be back at those drums, pal," said Jack. "Seriously, though, I think I speak for all of us, that we're glad you're ok. And, our many thanks to Dessa and Wendy for everything they did to make, what could have been a complete tragedy, turn out reasonably well. That is, with the exception of one broken leg and a shot-up wing."

Laughing, Wendy said, "It's all in the line of duty, Jack. That's why I get paid the big bucks. Catherine and Daisy are the ones we should be thanking more. If it wasn't for them, things might not have turned out this well."

"Yes, we all owe you a debt of gratitude. Thank you doesn't seem like enough for saving our lives, but that's all I have. And the same to you, Wendy. We would have never gotten this far without you." Letting go of Gene's hand, Judy went to Dessa's side and gave her a big hug. She said to her friend, "We have been like sisters since we were babies. You came with me on this journey to find my father, and you kept my spirits up when I was down and wanted to quit. And this is how you're repaid – you get shot. I'm so sorry about that. I owe you so much, Dessa. I love you." Blinking back the tears, she gave Dessa another hug and then went back to her dad.

"Judy, that's what friends are for. My arm doesn't hurt that bad, anyway," said Dessa, trying not to cry.

Clearing her throat, Catherine broke the silence, "Ok, that's enough of this. We should be happy now."

Just then, Detective Jacoby and Officer Svenson entered the room. They were greeted warmly by everyone.

Jack said, "Gentlemen, it's good to see you again. I believe we have a lot of questions to ask you. Things happened so quickly that we're all a little confused. Can you fill us in on the whole story?"

"I would like nothing better. This case has been going on for so long, that it's almost a letdown now that it's over. Why don't we sit over in the living room. Mr. Evans, are you able to join us?" asked Detective Jacoby.

"With help, I can. I'm going to have to get used to these crutches sometime." Gene leaned up, and Daisy helped him put on his robe and slippers, while Judy got his crutches ready. Slowly he managed to go over to a recliner and sat down, putting the footrest up so his leg would be supported.

He was lucky to have the private room that he had. Judy had made sure that he had the best room the hospital could provide. It had the usual section that all hospital rooms had, but then it had a sitting room area that included a bar with a mini frig. It also had a comfortable couch with matching side chairs and the recliner that Gene was now resting in. The colors of the room were blues, grays, and pale maroon. There were also side tables and a coffee table in a beautiful mahogany finish. Between the lamps and the room colors, the room was very cheery and conducive to a happy atmosphere. If you didn't know better, you'd think you were in a five-star hotel. Maintenance had brought in some extra folding chairs so that everyone could have a seat.

Catherine and Wendy got coffee and water for everyone, while Judy got a blanket and tucked it over Gene. When she did this, he looked at her with a combination of love and amazement. When everyone was settled, all eyes were on Detective Jacoby.

Clearing his throat, he started, "I told you this has been a long investigation, but I'll try to be as brief as possible. So, if you have any questions, just ask.

"Joseph Bradburn has been considered a shady character for several years now. Once he got to the executive department in Bradburn Pharmaceutical, and got some power, things seemed to change. Enough of a change that the SEC started getting suspicious. They have been carrying on a secret investigation ever since. "But they couldn't pinpoint anything. They finally came to our department and asked for our help. We put an undercover police woman in the company to help keep an eye on things. Miss Hensley has been Joseph Bradburn's personal assistant ever since." At this statement, Wendy, Judy, and Dessa looked at each other and grinned.

"When Charles Bradburn died suddenly, we knew we were on the right track, but we still couldn't prove anything. It seemed reasonable that he would have left everything to his only son, Joseph. When you came along, Miss Winslow, it was like holding a winning lottery ticket. Now all we had to do was find your father. Sounds simple, doesn't it? Let's backtrack a little. Remember, Miss Thornberry, when you were at Lucille Watkin's house and had some trouble?"

"Yes, Detective, I remember that quite well. I just figured I had been followed."

"We had staked out her house, thinking that someone might try to get to her for information. Guess who that was?" Detective Jacoby asked.

Dessa answered, "Lucas Barlow."

"You're absolutely right, Miss Stanton. But, we still didn't suspect him. After all, the reason he was there was to watch for trouble. What changed our minds was that he didn't call it in. We got the information from Wally. Even though there was plenty of time for Lucas to call in, he used time as an excuse. That's when something in my gut started to bother me.

"Then when he wanted to take a leave of absence because his mother was having emergency surgery back home in Colorado, I decided to follow him. That's when Officer Svenson and I picked you up. When we got to Arizona and followed you to Bubba's, we were watching from an alley when Lucas came outside and slashed the tires on your van.

"Up until then, I hoped that I was wrong. I've known that man since he entered the academy. I sorta took him under my wing, because I saw so much potential. I could have cried when I realized my gut was right. We knew that we had to keep an even closer eye on you ladies, so that nothing happened. We followed you to Los Angeles. You know the rest of the story on that."

Judy spoke up then and asked, "Detective, you were talking about my grandfather dying suddenly. What did you find out about that?"

"Joseph Bradburn's attorney, Stanley Nicols, was contacted. As soon as he knew about Barlow, he told us he wasn't going down alone. He told us that one night, Joseph smothered his father with a pillow. Not very imaginative, but effective. Nicols also kept a copy of the real will that Charles Bradburn had written. This will split everything he owned fifty-fifty between the two brothers. Mr. Nicols said that when Joseph Bradburn found out about this, he went ballistic. That's when he planned to find Mr. Evans, here, and take him out. He wasn't about to lose all that money that would go to you, Mr. Evans. But the power was even more important to him. He wasn't going to give that up, either.

"The district attorney had made an agreement with Mr. Nichols to turn state's evidence in exchange for immunity from prosecution. It has been decided that the man is pretty harmless, and, of course, won't be able to practice law ever again. So, it's worth it to get the goods on Joseph Bradburn. He'll be going away for a long time."

"Catherine, what part do you and Daisy play in all this?" asked Judy Catherine took over for Detective Jacoby. "When Charles Bradburn realized that Mr. Evans was his son, he wanted to take him into the business and treat him equal to his other son, Joseph. But, Mr. Evans had made it clear that he wanted to play in a band. So, Mr. Bradburn set up a trust fund for his older son. There was a security clause set up for you, Mr. Evans. There has been someone keeping track of you ever since the trust was written. There have been many people over the years who knew where you were and making sure you were ok. When the trustees found out that Joseph Bradburn officially knew about his brother, they decided to put a guard on you. That would be us."

Jack spoke up then, "How did you know that we would be needing a bass player? And are you and Daisy really sisters?"

With a sheepish look on her face, Catherine replied, "Yes, Daisy and I are really sisters. And she just happens to play the bass. That part is pure coincidence. The fact that you needed a bass player was taken care of by the trustees. We paid Dennis to leave and provided the cover story for him."

Again, Jack asked, "But what if we hadn't hired Daisy?"

This time it was Daisy who spoke, "How could you not? I'm really good!"

Everyone laughed at this. She was indignant, yet cute at the same time.

Gene said, "Catherine, I never wanted his money. He knew that. Why did he do this?"

"I don't know, but this might have the answers to your questions." Catherine pulled an envelope out of her purse. She got up and handed it to Gene. "This was written to you by your father. It was to be given to you at the discretion of the trustees. They sent it by overnight mail. Perhaps you'd like us to leave so you could read it in private."

"No, everyone here has the right to hear what the letter says. In fact, Judy, would you read it, please? I don't think I can." Gene's hand was shaking as he handed the envelope to Judy.

Opening the envelope, she recognized the writing from the previous letter that her grandfather had written. She took a deep breath and started to read.

'My dear son, Gene,

I wrote this letter to you when I set up your trust. I know that you don't want any of my money – you are a proud man. You remind me so much of myself when I was young. I wanted to do it all alone with nobody's help. I succeeded, but it was very difficult, indeed. Although I divided my estate between you and your half-brother, there were certain things that I left solely to him. *Things that I knew you wouldn't want, such as my house with its contents and the vehicles. He also will be making a great deal of money by his association with the Company. You will be getting cash and an equal number of shares of stock – not only in the Company, but in all my other investments. To help equalize the difference in the house, etc., I set up this trust for you. I have kept it a closely guarded secret. The trustees and those who they deem necessary are the only ones who know about this. I am having them keep track of you and report to me of your whereabouts. I, selfishly, want to know where you are and about your life. I, also, want to make sure you are safe. I don't want you to know of this until you read this letter. I don't want you to feel like a little boy who has to have his father hovering over him. As I said before, it is mostly because I love you so very much and crave as much information on your life as I possibly can get.*

Please remember that I loved your mother and wish that things could have been different with her. She never thought that she was good enough for me because she came from Poland. I never could convince her that not only was she good enough for me, but I felt she was better. I would have given up everything to have spent my life with her – and you. Always remember that.

I remain your loving Father'

Gene said, "I remember something now. When I was adopted, my new parents changed my last name from Wickovitch to their last name of Evans. They also changed my first name from Genek to Gene. They said that by doing that, it would make me feel like their real son. I guess I put that completely out of my mind."

Judy put the letter down in her lap and looked up at her father. He was crying, openly. She leaned over to hold him and cry along with him. The others, in the room, were all wiping their eyes and clearing their throats. Other than that, the room was quiet.

Finally, breaking the silence, Catherine said, "That's how I came into the picture."

"You said there have been people watching me over the years, but I've never noticed any one."

Catherine grinned and said, "Then I guess we did our job right."

This last statement broke the tension in the room, and people started talking and laughing with each other. After a few minutes, there came a knock at the door. Dessa answered it and let out a squeal of delight. Standing there were Judy's parents and hers. As they came into the room, Judy squealed, too, and rushed over to hold her parents, while Dessa was holding hers. They found themselves all talking at once. Finally, realizing that everyone else in the room was staring at them, introductions were made.

Judy's mother went to sit beside Gene and take his hand. Alexander motioned for the others to leave the room with him so that they could have some privacy.

After looking at her for a few minutes, Gene said, "Margaret, it's been a long time. You look as beautiful as ever. I owe you and Alexander my deepest thanks for taking such good care of our daughter. She seems to have turned out to be a lovely and kind, young woman. You must be very proud of her."

Margaret, smiling through her tears, said, "Yes, we are. She has always been a delight to us in every way. And it's us who should be thanking you for letting us raise her. I was distraught when I thought you had died. You can't imagine how I felt when I found out that you were alive. I was so happy about that. But, I was sad when I thought of how we had enjoyed Judith all these years, and you had never gotten any part of her."

"Please don't be upset about that. I chose to stay away. I didn't want to disrupt her life or yours. It was for the best. And my life hasn't been that bad. I've got my best friend, Jack, and the band. I can even say that I've found someone who will spend her life with me. At least, I think so. I guess I won't know until I ask her." With this, Gene laughed, and squeezed Margaret's hand.

Margaret smiled, put her arms around Gene, and gave him a kiss on the cheek. No other words were needed. They had mended things between them.

CHAPTER 35

WHEN THEY WENT into the hall, Dessa's parents were hovering around her. Her mother was dabbing at her eyes because 'her baby was hurt'. Her father just said, "Now, Mother. It's just a scratch, isn't it, Odessa?"

"Yes, Mom. Dad's right. It's nothing, really. I hurt myself worse when I scraped my leg falling off my bike. Please stop crying. I want you to meet the people who mean a lot to me. This is Wendy. She's the private detective without who we couldn't have found Judy's dad."

Wendy shook hands with Dessa's parents and Judy's father. "It's a pleasure to meet all of you. I've heard so much about you. As much as I like to take credit for things, the three of us worked together. Dessa and Judy did as much as anyone to get us here. You can be very proud of them."

Dessa then turned to Detective Jacoby and Officer Svenson and introduced them.

"These young women have been amazing," said Detective Jacoby. "Working with them really kept me on my toes."

Then Dessa turned to the other three, and as she introduced them said, "This is Jack, a dear friend to Gene. Catherine and Daisy are the ladies who saved our lives."

Judy, who was arm-in-arm with her father, looked up at him and said, "Thanks, Father, for making this all possible. I love you more than ever."

Her father just smiled and said, "I'm glad things turned out all right.

Your mother would have never forgiven me if they hadn't." Everyone laughed at that. "But, seriously, you deserved to know him."

Just then Margaret came to the door and invited them all to come back into the room. She and Gene both had a peaceful look on their faces. She went to her husband and gave him a kiss on the cheek and whispered to him, "Thank you, dear. Everything is all right."

Officer Svenson mentioned the time to Detective Jacoby, who said, "We have a plane to catch back to Miami. So we need to get going. Thank you for helping us clean up this case, and it was a pleasure to meet all of you. Let's go, Officer."

After the policemen left, Judy noticed that Gene was looking very tired. She said to Dessa, "I think we should go now. Gene needs to get some rest."

"I agree," said Dessa. "Gene, do you want to go back to bed or stay where you are?"

He answered, sleepily, "I think I'll just stay right here. This chair is pretty comfortable."

Alexander said, "I don't know about the rest of you, but I'm hungry. Let's go eat. Then you can catch us up on what has been going on. Sorry that you can't come with us, Gene. I'll have dinner sent over to you."

"Thanks, Alexander – for everything."

EPILOGUE

IT HAS BEEN several months since we found Judy's dad. It seems like as much has happened since that day as happened before that day.

Joseph Bradburn was tried and convicted for falsifying a legal document, embezzlement, second degree murder (the jury couldn't decide whether he had planned to kill his father or did it in the heat of the moment, so they went with the lesser of the two evils), and a number of other miscellaneous charges. He didn't take the verdict well. Dignity wasn't in the courtroom that day. They took him away kicking and screaming obscenities and threats at everyone.

Stanley Nichols was granted immunity in exchange for his testimony and was allowed to retire from his firm. He left Florida for parts unknown.

Gene's leg has healed nicely, and he's back on the road again with the band and his fiancé. Jack and Catherine are also engaged. They plan to marry in a double ceremony next year.

Daisy and Catherine are out of the security business. They weren't needed by the trustees any more, but they didn't care. Daisy is content with playing in the band. Catherine, who had always dabbled in finances, is now the manager of the band. She has proved her worth by getting them better and longer gigs.

Since Joseph was convicted of his crimes, all his assets went to Gene, who promptly turned over most of them to his daughter, Judy. Judy has taken over control of the Bradburn Pharmaceutical Company, with help from several major executives. It turns out that Joseph burnt a lot of bridges in his time as head of the Company. Everyone hated him. So they were more than happy to help educate her in the running of the business. The stockholders were so appalled at what had been going on with the Company, they were standing totally behind Judy.

Miss Hensley went back to the police force. She was promoted to detective.

Alexander and Margaret Winslow retired to Miami to be near Judy. They were closer than ever. Even Judy's grandmother decided to come with them. She got a condo in a building that was occupied by no one but senior citizens. She was actually happy.

As for me, well, Odessa Sue Stanton was now living in Miami and was a partner in the private investigative firm of Thornberry and Stanton. It took a lot of convincing, but Wendy kept at me until I gave in. My parents are still in Ohio, but they make trips to Florida often. It's just the three of us in the firm. Oh, did I forget to mention that our executive assistant is Lucille Watkins. She is great at what she does, and keeps us in line.

One last thing – Peter and Tim are still with the band. Nothing about what happened shook them up. They thought the whole thing (except the death of Lucas Barlow) was cool. Some things never change.

The End

Printed in the United States
By Bookmasters